One Night

Elite Escorts MM 1

Lynn Burke

One Night

I'm an Elite Escort in their new male on male branch, and the silver fox top role I play fulfills clients needing a little TLC in their everyday life. But being the one who constantly gives and never receives has me feeling drained.

When a voracious brat gets a taste of my wares, his obsession spirals out of control. I'm left floundering and needing someone to help me hold my head above water.

My secret desire comes to the rescue, and I feel like I can breathe for the first time in years.

Jasper is everything I've always wanted. From the outside, we look like a daddy and his boy when in reality he gives me what I need. It doesn't matter that he's smaller and a decade younger than me.

But the spoiled client isn't dissuaded from his pursuit, and I'm faced with having to unearth truth that will have dire consequences.

Will the wounds he inflicted prove too much to overcome? Or will Jasper's determination to show me my inner strength help me weather a storm capable of ruining every-thing—everyone—I love?

Prologue

Mason

"Do I even want to know?"

I considered my sister's question before answering. She was aware of the job I'd lost, but I hadn't shared with her the contract I'd signed a couple weeks earlier to help keep her head—and her family's—above water.

"It's nothing illegal," I assured her, my insides quaking.

That was what my new boss had assured me of anyway.

"Nothing that will put you in harm's way?" Marin's concern bled through her tone, but she'd always been the nurturer to my older, softer soul.

"Promise." I wasn't sure I lied, but I had hopes for the night and months ahead. The amount of money I would make with every booking offered me the chance to assist her as I hadn't been able to before. Climbing out of my car, I took my cell off speaker and held it up to my ear. "I have to go, Sis. Give your boys hugs from Uncle Mason."

"When are you going to fly your sorry ass out here and hug them yourself?"

I considered my bank account that always sat on the

verge of empty. "This new job pays better, so someday soon."

"You'd better. It's been too damn long," Marin muttered in my ear. "Love you, big bro."

"Love you too. I'll transfer some money to you next week, okay?"

"You're the best." Marin's voice broke. "I don't know what I'd do without you."

"You would survive—same as we've always done." I hung up a few seconds later, swallowing thickness from my throat. Thoughts of family and love had no place in my mind for the coming hours.

Shoving my phone in my back pocket, I headed toward the hotel's entrance, my heart rate quickening. While I couldn't have much planned out in advance for my evening, I knew what to expect: a young man close to my height. Closet case. Strict bottom.

The cash would be well worth stepping outside my comfort zone with that last bit of knowledge and allow me to pay off one of my nephew's medical bills and help provide for my sister's family. That truth sent relief racing through my bloodstream, easing some of my jitters.

I counted to slow my breathing while riding the elevator to the eighth floor, my palm sweating where I clutched tightly to a black bag. I would do what I had to do—same as I always did.

My knock beneath the #816 plate echoed through the hallway.

Please the client.

The words repeated in my head as Preston pulled open the door to the suite he'd booked for the night. We stood eye to eye at just shy of six feet like I'd expected, his curls flaming red and gold beneath the dim overhead light. His focus flitted from my prematurely graying hair and beard to my fitted slacks and back up, lingering briefly on the olive button-down shirt that made my hazel eyes more sea-like than muddy.

"Mason?" he asked, finally settling his wary yet interested gaze on my face. The green of his orbs was even more stunning in person than on his profile picture.

I smiled easier than I'd expected, hoping to help him relax when my insides danced probably twice as fast as his. "Yes."

He swallowed hard and stepped aside, allowing me entrance.

I'd never been in a swanky hotel before and took a quick glance around the space while setting aside the bag. My gaze got caught up on the windows overlooking Boston's night skyline. Quite the view, one I hadn't seen from such a height.

But a lot of firsts lay ahead of me tonight.

Preston would break my cherry so to speak, and as his escort, it was up to me to make him comfortable. Bring him pleasure in whatever way he wished. Fulfill his desires listed in the file I'd received from Elite Escort MM's secretary, even if they didn't match up with my own.

To say nervousness raced through my system would be an understatement, but I couldn't help my excitement at a new, lucrative beginning.

"Would you like a drink?" Preston's voice wavered, and I turned to find him wringing his hands in front of him. He'd gone barefoot, wore loose jeans, and a T-shirt stretched over his hitched shoulders.

While the young man's handsomeness couldn't be denied, he lacked the twink-like build I preferred. But getting him to relax and find release was my responsibility, and I wasn't about to let him or my new boss down.

"Are you having one?" I asked even though I wouldn't have minded something to help settle myself as well.

"I-I'm not sure?"

I smiled wider, my heart going out to the kid I found myself identifying with—a lot. "How about we just sit on the couch and cuddle a little bit instead? You look like you could use a hug more than anything right now."

Fuck knew I could.

Rather than leading me into the sitting area at my suggestion, Preston exhaled until his shoulders slumped and walked straight into me, laying his cheek on my shoulder, his nose in my neck.

I wrapped my arms around him as he did the same, and I closed my eyes, soaking in the warmth, the simple affection I hadn't experienced in far too long. Preston might not be able to offer me what I longed for, but I would earn every dollar he had dished out for gratification.

Silence hovered over the suite, but something about the young man set my frayed inner self at ease, creating a tranquil quietness between us. His hot breath on my neck sent a shiver down my spine, and the slight shift of his hips rubbed his hard-on against me.

At least he found my body arousing—and vice versa. That would hopefully make my job easier.

I slid my hands down over the curve of his ass, pulling him tighter against me. The promise of feeling warm skin and muscle was enough to interest my dick beyond the pill I'd taken to ensure I wouldn't have any issues in giving Preston what he'd paid for.

He shuddered in a way I recognized, and I set my mind on meeting his needs for the night.

"Let me take care of you?" I murmured before pressing a kiss to his forehead.

Stepping back, he kept his focus on the floor and nodded. He grasped my hand, his palm clammy against mine as he started toward the open double doors, revealing a king-sized bed beyond.

The file from Elite I'd read through—four times in the previous twenty-four hours due to anxiety—assured me that Preston wasn't a virgin, but I wondered over his experience. His body language screamed careful to a fault, the same sort of inner timidity I'd taken on as a child and hadn't ever been able to free myself from. But I had fifteen if not twenty years on Preston and had learned to don a mask that hid the many ways I lacked.

I'd expected to lead throughout our time together, but Preston stopped before the bed and began undressing me like a gift he wished to savor. I soaked in the attention, thrilled by his touch. His slow, shaky movements stripped me down to my black boxer briefs, and for those few moments, I gloried in finding satisfaction in a job I'd been unsure of. My chest squeezed even as my heart attempted to burst free from my body.

"Show me what it's like," he murmured, finally lifting his focus to my face.

I cupped his smooth-shaven cheek, rubbing my thumb over his plump lower lip.

He sighed and leaned into my hand as though he was as touch starved as I was. We were far from sexually compatible, but I led, offering him everything, as though I was the one on the receiving end.

Gentle kisses while stripping him of his pants and briefs.

Soothing caresses to every inch of his freckled skin I bared from the waist up.

I found his erogenous zones, lingering at the base of his neck with licks and nibbles. He arched beneath me as I loved on his tightly furled nipples, his leaking dick smearing pre-cum on my abs.

His whimpers and pleas to be filled with my dick would have made most gay men impossibly hard, but were it not for that little blue pill, I would have flagged—disappointed the man who'd paid for the use of my body.

A needy boy, Preston soaked up everything I offered, begging for more.

My mouth.

My fingers.

My dick.

I gave him all three, but it was awhile before he was ready for my girth. It took an even longer time for me to breach his ring and finally bottom out inside his tight heat.

He kept his eyes closed while I rearranged his guts, but I didn't demand he look at me so he knew who owned his ass in that moment. What was the point of getting involved on an emotional level especially when we weren't really compatible? I had been paid to fuck him, not connect with him.

I couldn't help but relate though as he grasped at my back with desperate fingers. Wrapped his legs around my waist and begged me for more—harder. Deeper.

I did as told, but it was my mouth offering praise, telling him how well he took every inch of me when my ears burned to hear similar words.

Preston gulped, his eyelids blinking open to meet my gaze. The young man was drunk on lust, panting, his eyes glazed over. His hard cock lay trapped between our bodies, pre-cum a smeared mess on our skin.

"C-Close," he stuttered before letting out a small, needy whine.

I shifted onto my haunches and wrapped my fist around his rigid length.

"Oh—Oh God." He watched me work him in time with my thrusts, whimpers pouring from his parted lips to battle the lewd sounds of fucking with too much lube. "Right there...oh shit, I'm gonna—"

Copious amounts of cum shot up over his chest, splattering as far as his mouth. His tight ring clasped with pulsing contractions around my dick. Bliss rushed across his face as he licked his lips clean and continued to convulse beneath me.

I'd brought him euphoric pleasure, but even that truth didn't cause my own climax.

I imagined myself in Preston's place. A thick dick stretching my hole, the fullness and hard thrusts over my prostate making me squirm with desperation. Crooned words of approval while a spurting cock prolonged my pleasure.

My ass clenched with need.

I groaned while filling the condom, shutting out all thoughts so I could enjoy my unexpected release. A final shudder wracked my body, and I slumped onto my elbows, my forehead dropping to Preston's shoulder as I struggled to catch my breath.

I'd done it. Brought my client to climax—and even had one of my own. Relief swept through me, doubling my coming down.

Preston's smooth hands slid along my spine to my backside where he squeezed. "Thank you."

"Glad to be of service," I murmured, smiling as he laughed lightly. I pulled out of his tight clasp, keeping hold of the condom.

He grimaced, and I kissed the inside of his thigh, trying to remember what it felt like to be uncomfortably empty and deliciously sore.

It had been too damn long.

"Be right back," I murmured, pushing against sudden melancholy wanting to rob me of the bit of pleasure I'd found with my client.

Aftercare was expected, and Preston seemed to appreciate me taking the time to ensure he was comfortable after the pounding I'd given him.

"Did I hurt you?" I asked, tossing the washcloth aside.

"No. Your big dick was exactly what I needed."

Satisfaction should have risen up inside my chest. My ego should have swelled. I definitely should have grinned. None of those things happened, but I shoved the thoughts away and told myself to accept what was—not dream about what I would never find.

"Will you stay with me?" Preston asked, once more seeming a bit unsettled with how his gaze flitted over my face.

Perhaps I'd lingered too long sitting on the edge of the bed, lost in my head rather than paying attention to the man who'd hired me through Elite. Setting aside selfishness, I refixed the mask I wore and focused on my *job*. Pleasing my client.

"Of course I will." I slid between the sheets, gathering Preston into my arms as he snuggled against me. He had me until eight the next morning, and I reminded myself to be whatever he wished for in the hours ahead of us. Thankfully, my time with him included snuggling I expected some clients might not accept or even appreciate.

First came pillow talk, or rather a willing ear to simply listen.

I hadn't known therapist was one of the titles I would wear as an escort. I'd expected to simply be eye candy. A hungry mouth for those who wanted to be sucked off. A hard dick they could impale themselves on. Possibly a greedy hole on the rare occasion a client desired to top the silver fox daddy I'd been showcased as on Elite Escort MM's website.

A man could hope...

Preston shared with me how he was deeply closeted thanks to his mother. His biological father had transitioned and went by the name of Nancy not long after his parents had divorced. Preston had been a young teenager battling over his own sexual preferences at the time. His mother refused to accept her ex's identity and continued to drop homophobic bullshit years later. So, Preston chose to live a lie.

The fact he could afford EEMM ensured me the guy had cash to spare, but he struggled to find himself and create the future he dreamed of. Going through the motions meant depression he took medication for and a struggle to find happiness in life.

I related all too well, wanting to offer him an opportunity to forget and simply *be*.

And fuck if those feelings didn't sting like hell knowing I would once again be on the giving end.

"This was my first time hiring someone like you," he said, still wrapped up in my arms. "I-I don't mean that in a demeaning way—I don't judge people for how they make a living. There's nothing wrong with being a sex worker. Shit. I hope you understand what I'm trying to say."

"I do," I assured him, my body still while inner restlessness made me want to finish out my hours so I could escape the conflicting emotions Preston roused inside me. Pleasure. Satisfaction in knowing I could send Marin more money. Bummed I wouldn't get the dick or aftercare I yearned for.

"You won't...talk about this with anyone, will you?" Preston asked. "I signed the NDA, but that applies to you too, right?"

"That's correct."

Preston pulled back to study my face. "And you don't bullshit about clients with the other escorts? Like, you don't go out for drinks with your coworkers and share stories about the guys desperate enough to dish out major bucks to get laid in secret?"

"You're safe with me—and Elite. Promise." And he was. Confidentiality for all parties was one of EEMM's top requirements. My boss demanded it, ensured a mere word of information leaked would see our employment contract torn to pieces and asses sued.

Preston released a huge sigh. "Good. The last thing I need is that asshole finding out I'm gay and telling my mom."

"What asshole?" I asked, pushing some of his thick hair off his forehead since he was touch starved. He blossomed beneath my hands.

He smiled, his eyelids falling shut at the caress.

I kept up with the soft caresses over his smooth skin, moving forward according to his sighs and shifts.

"My stepbrother—he's an Elite."

I paused in my exploration of his happy trail and slender dick once more dripping for attention. "What?"

"Nothing." He huffed a laugh, his cheeks flushing. "Forget it—never mind. Just keep...touching me like that."

Well, shit.

I didn't know any other of the escorts employed by EEMM except for one, my friend who'd gotten me the job, and his parents were still happily married.

While I wanted to ask Preston about his stepbrother, I expected it was safer for both of us if I dropped the conversation for good.

I slid down the front of his body and set to work emptying his balls a second time in a way I would thoroughly enjoy. Working for Elite offered me the kind of money I needed, and I wasn't about to allow a client's family, his past, or my own desires fuck up a good thing when others relied on me to pay their bills.

Settling between Preston's spread thighs, I earned every penny.

And he thanked me again with a smile on his face before falling asleep with his cheek against my chest.

Chapter 1

Mason

Six Months Later...

Only a few months of working for Elite, and my mask of confidence had started to slip.

I was the best at playing the silver daddy-type a lot of clients hungered for and earned my boss Micah Fox a shit ton of cash every week. Words of praise over a job well done from both him and those I took care of had given me a sense of satisfaction after that first night with Preston, but greedy bottoms had started to suck me dry.

And not in the good way.

Add in the bullshit I'd dealt with due to a different returning client two weeks earlier, and—

A shiver slid down my spine, raising the hairs on my neck. Releasing a heavy exhale, I shut my eyes and attempted to shove away the traumatic memory and focus on where I stood rather than imagining that sick fuck watching me from the shadows.

I was at the Sweet Water Suite at one of Boston's finest hotel's, celebrating my boss's fortieth birthday.

A half-empty tumbler of Grey Goose on the rocks cooled my palm.

Air conditioning blasted, keeping the late July's humidity at bay and allowing me to be comfortable in my tight jeans and button-down.

Steady thumps sounded from speakers in the far corner bracketing the event's DJ, but even the upbeat music didn't help me overcome my conflicting thoughts concerning that horrific night with one of Elite's highest-paying customers.

It hadn't been the first time the rich brat had bought an evening with me and my dick, but it *would* be the last. The kid had fucked me over to the point I should have called the cops or at least gone to the hospital.

But pressing charges would have only brought about a shitstorm for me and Elite, so I'd kept the entire affair to myself.

The last thing I needed to do was stir up a hornet's nest and cause problems for Micah, especially since his escort service barely skirted the edge of legal in the state of Massachusetts.

The client wasn't just some bored computer programmer nerd who couldn't land a hookup on an app either. His father was a well-known man in Boston and beyond. Deep pockets due to his family name promised that going after him would bring devastation in ways I had zero wish to even think about let alone relive in court.

I gently probed at the tender spot atop my heart, hating the fact an actual scar would linger along with nightmares from that night.

At least Micah hadn't questioned my requesting a few days off afterward, then bowing out from taking on that same rapacious twink three nights ago when he'd attempted to book with me again.

No fucking way would I—

"Hey."

I blinked my eyes open to find my good friend Kellen beside me. He wore a dark suit coat over his equally black button-down and form-fitting jeans that hugged his thick thighs and calves. A strong jawline, artfully mussed hair... the man was gorgeous but way too tall and muscular for my liking.

"You okay?" he asked, his hazel-green eyes flicking over my face with concern.

I put on my cocksure smile as always when in public, not for the first time seriously jealous over his lack of gray hair. He was only a couple of years younger than my forty-two but had aged better than I had.

"Yeah. Just tired," I lied, my tone intentionally light.

Like me, Kellen was an EEMM employee. He'd been the one to introduce me to Micah when I'd lost my job in business management earlier that year. Since I'd been down to my last penny and Marin needed cash, I'd jumped at the chance to escort men around. Being eye candy. Giving blow jobs, offering up my ass if that was what they preferred. An easy way to get dicked down without any effort on my part.

But I'd gotten cast as a top due to the daddy vibes Micah swore he picked up on during my interview. Desperate for work, I'd learned to hide my desire to be taken care of and ended up being the giver.

Every. Time.

And one *taker* had shaken the foundation of my livelihood.

Kellen grabbed hold of my elbow, keeping my mind from drifting any further. "I've known you long enough to recognize when you're full of it, Mason. Don't feed me your bullshit. What's going on?"

Slowly emptying my lungs, I considered puking up all the words I'd kept bottled inside me forever. But emotions would release along with my explanation, and if I'd learned anything from my childhood with a manipulative narcissist, it was self-preservation.

"Just tired," I repeated, hoping like hell Kellen would let it go.

He didn't respond, and I scanned the room. I hadn't pushed Preston about his stepbrother during the two other nights I'd been hired by him since our first time together, nor had I figured out who the guy might be. Dozens of current employees attended Micah's party, but former Elites who had found love and solid connections with their partners were also sprinkled throughout the crowd.

Blake and his wife Wren shared a private moment in the shadows, eyes only for one another. Reid and Jessie, on a date night without their two kids, appeared exhausted but smiled while holding hands. Jarod's flame-haired firecracker of a woman on his arm peered at him like he hung the moon in the sky.

Lucky dogs—all of them, but at one time, they had probably felt like menu items too.

Preston was a client who didn't make me feel that way. Perhaps because he'd been my first and truly appreciated me, or maybe because I'd come to care for his well-being after hours of listening to him unload his worries.

Either way, he was the booking I looked forward to the most every month—and not because of the sex.

If only we were well-matched in the bedroom...

Kellen slung an arm over my shoulders and gave me a side bro-hug. "I'm here if you need to talk."

I soaked in the rare bit of affection but pulled away long before I had my fill. "Ready for another drink?" I asked, nodding toward his almost emptied tumbler, surprised my voice sounded upbeat considering how unsteady my insides were over the nightmare client who'd haunted my dreams the previous couple of weeks.

"Sure."

We weaved through the crowd for the bar, the base of my neck once more tingling.

Ever since the night with that voracious twink, I'd been on high alert. Jumpy and suspicious. A fucking anxious mess I struggled to keep contained. Without the help of those pills Elite supplied, I never would have been able to please the couple of clients I'd been booked with since him.

A group of guys snagged us while en route to refill our drinks, their natural jollity pulling my mood even lower. I smiled brighter in response, a master at hiding my true self thanks to good old Mom.

I needed a fucking break.

Or a million bucks so I could get my sister out of debt and whisk myself away on a cruise to the Cayman Islands where problems didn't exist.

Huffing a snort at myself, I attempted to focus on the story Sean, Elite's MM manager and Micah's much younger brother, told about the guy who had railed his ass the night before. The blond-haired, blue-eyed cutie wasn't just in charge of Elite's gay branch but gladly took on clients as well.

He had been an out-and-proud frat boy back in his college days and had zero plans on settling down anytime soon. He also wasn't shy about his hunger for dick and how long he'd been after his brother to expand Elite to include a smorgasbord for him to gorge on.

"He was so deep up my ass I could feel him in the back of my throat."

I grimaced at Sean's description of the client's length. Give me girth any day of the week.

"What?" Sean asked me with a laugh when he caught sight of my face.

My cheeks heated over feeling all four men peer at me, and I forced a slow, cocky upturn of my lips. "I don't like having my guts rearranged."

Drake, another of Elite's employees, clasped my shoulder, his blue eyes full of laughter. "It's a good thing you're an exclusive top."

"Damn right." I winked on autopilot after so many months of playing my part.

Drake peered at me intently, making my laughter fade. "You okay, man?" he asked.

Grin still in place, I nodded with surety. "All good."

He sipped his beer while continuing to study me as though knowing I spoke out of my ass.

"Ever get complaints about that python in your pants?" Sean asked me, and I latched onto the opportunity to turn Drake's concern away from digging any deeper.

"Not a goddamn one," I allowed but wouldn't brag about the truth.

Clients tended toward the opposite, asking me to give them more. How some of them took all of me, I had no clue. I'd have been perfectly content to never shove my cock into another greedy hole ever again.

"I'm calling bullshit—we've all heard about your massive dick," Sean pushed, still laughing. He'd had a bit too much to drink if his slightly slurred words were any indication. "You know what we should do?"

Drake groaned and tipped back his beer for a long swallow as though well aware of where Sean's thoughts headed. The two men had been close friends since childhood, but from what I'd seen countless times, Drake tended to be the responsible party when they got together.

Sean loved to tease and had zero fucking filter. The brat needed a real daddy with a heavy hand.

"Let's whip them out and measure!" Sean said.

Kellen snorted a laugh and shook his head.

Sean's drink-hazed eyes blazed with excitement while Drake rolled his. "Yeah, I don't think your brother would appreciate that." His best friend stated a fact.

"Ah." Sean waved his hand dismissively while snorting. "Fuck Micah."

"No thanks," Drake mumbled.

"If my uptight brother wanted to really bring in the dough," Sean continued, "he'd highlight *exactly* what Elite's men have on offer rather than us clothed from the waist down. Pretty pink holes and big dicks are always in high demand."

So were silver fox daddies. Elite needed to hire another to spread the load I'd been carrying all on my own the previous six months.

"You know he can't showcase that shit, asshole," Drake muttered.

"He needs a couple of twinks in the lineup too," Sean continued, ignoring Drake. Blatantly offering cocks and asses would end Elite and leave a lot of men jobless.

I'd had enough talk of holes, dicks, and fucking. Catching Kellen's eye, I gestured with my head toward the bar.

He nodded and clasped Sean's shoulder, cutting him off mid-sentence. "We'll be back in a bit. Gonna go grab a drink."

Sean hollered after us to get him another beer. "One for my man Drake too!"

Snickering, Kellen gave him a thumbs up and fell into step beside me. "Those two put more beer away than any guy I know."

He didn't lie.

At least Drake could hold his alcohol. The man tended toward quiet, the strong, silent type—Sean's opposite. While Sean had muscle on his lean frame, Drake hit the gym and weights with the intention to stay bulked up. At six-two, he had quite a few inches on his best friend, easily carrying the mass of muscle he'd gained. And unlike Sean's baby face, Drake kept a full beard neatly clipped along his strong jawline.

I scratched at my own prematurely graying whiskers, wondering if maybe shaving would change my image.

But what client would want a gray-haired dude sans the popular facial hair that made him look like the silver fox daddy they desired to spend a night with?

Maybe it was time for a new job.

"What are you drinking?" Kellen asked me as we sidled up to the bar.

"Just a tonic with lime this time around." The last thing I needed was more vodka adding to my maudlin mood.

Kellen gave our orders, and I once more checked out the crowd to see if anyone was worth sticking around for when my bed begged me to come home and crash.

Blake was easily the most known in the room outside of Elite's owner. The dude was loaded and, because of his grandfather being a senator or something, was considered a *who's who* of Boston's higher society.

A giant of a redhead with a curvy brunette tucked under his arm stood talking with Blake and Wren. On Blake's other side, a woman holding a glass of champagne appeared well-acquainted with Botox and seemed awfully fond of black leather. Her lips were puffy and obscene, and the corset encasing her waist accented the mass of tits threatening to spill free.

She didn't exactly...*fit in* even though close to half of the crowd was rumored to be kinky as fuck and either employed by Elite or had been at one time.

"Who's the woman?" I asked as Kellen handed me my drink.

"The busty blonde talking with Blake and Cooney?"

Daniel Cooney—that was the huge guy's name. He'd been an Elite too, until he went and fell in love too. I sipped my ice-cold drink, wishing it soothed my jealousy as well as it did my warm insides.

"Yeah."

"That's Mistress Chantelle."

I took a second to process Kellen's offered information. "As in Chantelle's—the BDSM club?"

"That's the one." Kellen nodded. "Cooney has something to do with the shibari classes there or used to anyway. Pretty sure Micah and his wife play at the club on occasion too."

I'd heard Micah was a heavy-handed Dom and used to be on Elite's menu for when a submissive came looking for a little pain with their pleasure. To each their own and all that shit, but I had no interest in that sort of lifestyle.

We stood a few moments, watching the crowd and enjoying our drinks.

I noted Kellen held two bottles of beer in his hand. "Taking those to Sean and Drake?" I asked, deciding I'd had enough pretending and was ready to bail and escape the crowd and noise.

"Yeah."

I set my tonic on the bar behind me. "I'm going to head out."

Kellen once more gave me that questioning stare. "Sure you're okay, Mason?"

I grinned and added a cocky tip upward to my chin. "Client last night drained me in more ways than one." It was hardly the truth physically, but the charade I played neared its end for the night. "You're traveling to Maine in the morning, right?" I asked, intentional as fuck in redirecting his thoughts.

"Yeah. Getting up early so I can be there for my mom's birthday breakfast."

"Don't stay too late, then." I clasped his shoulder. "I'll see you later."

Kellen let me go with a simple nod, his eyes telling me I hadn't fooled him.

I skirted my way around the ballroom's edge, ready to head home and bury myself in my pillows, but paused beside Micah who still chatted with Cooney.

"Happy fortieth," I offered while clasping my boss's hand. "It's all downhill from here."

"Thanks." He snickered but did a quick study of my face, his pale eyes concerned—and too damn intuitive, especially with my usual ability to bullshit flagging. "You're leaving already?"

I managed to hold my grin in place. "Yeah—I'm beat."

Micah gave me a raised eyebrow that suggested he wanted to call me out, but he didn't, thank fuck.

Cooney clasped my shoulder in his meaty paw. "Take it easy, Mason. Get some rest. Looks like you need it."

"Well thanks," I shot back, trying for a snarky attitude I didn't feel.

A few minutes later, I breathed a sigh of relief while making my way toward one of the hotel's side exits closest to the parking garage.

Humid, too-hot air hit me like a brick wall as I stepped out into the dark alleyway. Exhaust and the scent of a restaurant's grill filled my nose. A horn honked, and engines revved from the main road to my left.

The door snicked shut behind me, and I tipped my head back, eyes closed against the night while wishing I was anywhere but downtown Boston.

I longed for the scent of salt water and suntan oil. Exotic flowers and ozone after a storm like we'd had earlier in the day. The city's air didn't carry the freshness rain usually brought but a damp heaviness that matched the weariness hovering over my shoulders.

A dozen or so hours of sleep would help. Then coffee. I would make myself some waffles covered in strawberries and whipped cream after a second cup—that always did the trick.

Mind set on my bed, I started across the narrow alley, trying to remember which floor of the parking garage I'd left my car.

The door I'd escaped through snicked open and shut behind me, and the scuff of quick feet on the road made me turn my head on instinct.

A blur of black flashed in my periphery.

"What—"

Something slammed into the side of my head, ripping the word from me as I stumbled to my side, landing on my knees. Ears ringing and vision swimming, I attempted to crawl forward and escape whoever had jumped me.

"Fuck! H-Help!" I hollered, gravel digging into my palms and knees as I tried to scurry forward on limbs refusing to cooperate.

A stinging swipe slashed across my shoulder, jacking my heartrate up even further.

I yelled another curse while curling in on myself. "I-I have money in my wallet! Take it! Please don't hurt me!"

A boot to my ribs radiated pain through my core, ripping another cry from my lungs and flooding my mind with fear—the instinctive need to get away.

Rolling, I lifted my arms, trying to shield my face from my attacker as another kick got me in the gut. I groaned, and something solid once more hit my head in the same goddamned spot as the first blow.

Darkness hovered at the edge of my mind, wanting to swoop in and swallow me whole.

"Hey!" A voice rang out in the distance.

Footfalls raced away...others toward me.

Numbness crept through my limbs even as my head throbbed, and I struggled to make out the night sky.

I welcomed the threatening unconsciousness.

Chapter 2

Jasper

He didn't show.

Heart heavy, I slid off my stool, ready to escape the hotel's loud, obnoxious atmosphere. A few events took place in the ballrooms, and partiers had migrated into the bar area where I'd been waiting for my date.

Supposedly, the man I'd been chatting with online for the previous couple of weeks had a room on the third floor, but we'd agreed to meet up downstairs since both of us weren't just looking for a quick fuck and run.

We'd found each other through an online dating service meant to connect gay men with their soulmates. He'd seemed decent enough, we got along without stilted conversations over the phone, and more importantly, he'd claimed to be my perfect match in the bedroom. Something I'd always had trouble with since my outward appearance didn't match most people's idea of what a top ought to look like.

And finding a larger man who was confident enough in himself to allow a smaller, more feminine guy to be the leader, the caretaker in a relationship? Damn near impossible.

While I hadn't gone so far as to wear a pink dress shirt like I'd have preferred beneath my suit coat, my expectations for the night had remained high. I had allowed myself to be hopeful when past attempts at finding my person should have taught me better.

I'd been nothing but a failure since childhood.

My father offered love and acceptance—as long as I didn't act like the faggot femme boy I was at heart. His flesh and bones rotted six feet under, but I was still stuck beneath his influence, unable to free myself from the strain of never being enough. I'd hoped a love match would help heal my soul-deep wounds that still festered, but I would forever keep my secret desires locked up even if I ever did find a man I connected with.

Lips in a thin line over my latest failure in finding *the one*, I headed toward the bar's rear exit. I couldn't put through a call to my date amidst the noise, and he hadn't answered either of the texts I'd sent in the previous thirty minutes.

Maybe something had happened and he had a good reason for not showing. A few excuses ran through my head, including emergency phone calls from loved ones. Maybe he'd fallen asleep after arriving at the hotel from his long cross-country flight for a work meeting in Boston the following Monday. Perhaps he'd ordered room service for an early dinner and had choked to death.

That final scenario amused me regardless of my bitter disappointment.

Muggy darkness hovered over Boston's sky when I stepped out into the night, stopping my mind from thinking of more possible causes as to why I'd been stood up. I jerked my tie loose while fumbling with my phone in my other hand. I would allow my date one last chance to answer my call.

A door to my left slammed—another suited guy had stepped outside, cell in hand, his dark hair slicked back. Unfortunately, he looked like an Italian mob boss, not the blond I'd been waiting for.

Ignoring Mr. Mafia Dude manly-man, I clicked on contacts. I'd never had trouble finding hookups with twinks when I'd grown bored with my hand, but for once, I had thought I stood a chance of having a bigger man beneath me. Why couldn't I get lucky for a change?

Someone hollered close by—a curse and call for help.

The mobster beside me took off for the building's corner toward an alleyway where the ruckus had come from, and always the protective one, I followed on his heels, almost losing my loafers in my rush to keep up.

A slim person dressed in dark clothes stood over a man curled into a fetal position on the road.

"Hey!" I shouted, jerking the attacker's head our way. They wore a ski mask, but even without the covering, I wouldn't have been able to make them out in the alleyway's darkness.

They took off in the opposite direction. Mafia Dude beside me gave chase.

"Hey, Siri!" I hollered, my cell in hand. "Call 911!"

An operator answered immediately, muffled and not on speaker.

I yelled out about the attack and my location while running toward the man on the asphalt.

Blood seeped from a wound on his head, the skin around it already swelling. Keeping the operator on the line,

I set my phone down on the ground close by so I could tend to the man with both of my hands.

Cursing quietly, I tore off my pristine suit coat that even my dad would have approved of and pressed it against the fallen man's laceration near his temple. "I called 911. It's going to be okay," I told him in a soothing voice, not sure if he heard me with how dazed he appeared.

Footfalls sounded—the mobster approached.

I opened my mouth to ask about the attacker, but unmistakable pops sounded from inside the hotel, making me hover over the man beside me. Hollers followed in the gun's wake, and my heart rate went from rapid to frantic.

Mafia Dude's head whipped back the way we'd come. "Shit! I have family inside. Are you okay to stay with him?"

What the fuck?

Gulping, I nodded, watching him sprint away. Had those actually been *real* gunshots? Maybe it had been a car backfiring—

The man in front of me groaned, and I turned back around. "Help will be here soon," I tried to assure him.

Remembering the call I hadn't ended, I glanced at my cell on the road beside me. It remained active. I grabbed it up in my free hand and hurriedly explained what I'd heard from inside the hotel while glancing around us. What if another masked person or someone with a gun in hand headed our way? Sirens rose in the distance before I'd even finished telling the operator what had gone down.

Setting my cell aside again, I gave the wounded man my full attention once more.

"It's going to be okay," I promised even though I spoke out of my ass. "You're going to be just fine. My name is Jasper, and I'll be here with you until the cops show up. You aren't alone."

He blinked, his hazel eyes seeming to latch onto mine with desperation. Fear and pain radiated from him as though his soul cried out for someone to save him.

The sirens faded from my awareness. My pulse thrummed in my ears. Like a poignant moment in a movie, time slowed, and warmth spread through my veins alongside the anxiousness from our situation.

The man clasped my wrist. Heat from his touch zapped through me like a live electrical volt, jolting my groin. "I'm M-Mason," he rasped his name, his lips barely moving.

He had quite a few years on me...late-forties, maybe? A sexy silver fox with a strong jawline covered by a groomed, graying beard. A grimace curled one corner of his lips, and I pushed aside thoughts of how soft his whiskers would feel on my skin...how perfectly he fit my daydreams of happily-ever-afters. By appearances, at least. God knew I'd seen hundreds of such men in my time only to be disappointed to learn they wouldn't bottom for a guy like me.

Clearing my throat, I glanced down over his trim but muscular body. He wore a dark green button-down stretched over wide shoulders and tight-fitting jeans that left absolutely nothing to the imagination. Thick thighs suggested he spent time in the gym, and a bulge worthy of drool ensnared my gaze. My mind wandered into instantaneous lust and the fact I hadn't felt fulfilled sexually in far too long.

Focus on the present, you twit.

I forced my gaze back on Mason's face, once more struck by his eyes emanating a sense of being lost, as though he was adrift and in need of someone of help him tread water. My instincts kicked in.

"Where else are you hurt?" I asked, awareness of our surroundings returning to include the noise around us.

Sirens taxed my ears, echoing through the alleyway, and flashes of blue and red lit the sky, but no cops had arrived on the scene.

Mason's grimace remained. "I—I'm not sure?"

The attacker had a knife...

"Did he stab you?" I asked, once more doing a quick scan of Mason's body.

"My shoulder." Mason still clasped my wrist, his focus on my eyes. "Hurts."

"I got you." I cradled his neck with my free hand, hoping to help steady him. The warmth of his skin seeped into my palm, snaking its way up my arm and toward my chest. "Help will be here soon."

Cops appeared at the alleyway's entrance, guns drawn. "Hands up!" one hollered. "Get your hands up where we can see them!"

I tore my fingers from Mason's nape but kept the other hand against his temple. "I'm putting pressure on this man's head wound!" I called back, my heart racing. "He was attacked and is bleeding."

"Don't move!" An officer approached hesitantly, gun trained on me, and I shivered, my stomach clenching up tight. He got close enough he could see I spoke the truth, and he barked orders to get an EMT to our location immediately.

I gave Mason my full focus, our gazes once more locking. "You're going to be okay."

The pain in his eyes remained, but he continued to cling to my wrist as though afraid letting go would send him adrift once more.

"I have you, Mason. Promise," I whispered, wanting nothing more than to soothe the gorgeous man who'd been thrust into my life.

It seemed hours later that two men arrived to care for Mason, and I grabbed my cell and moved slightly off to the side to give them room to work. My ears strained as I fought to listen to Mason answer questions about where he hurt. His gaze kept flitting my way, making my entire body ache to crowd in close—to be near to him.

Once strapped to a gurney, Mason held his hand out toward me as though he sensed the same draw.

His need hauled me in like a well-greased pulley, and I found myself reaching for him. Our palms clasped, fingers entwined, sending that volt through me once more.

"Can I come along to the hospital?" I asked the EMT readying to roll Mason up the alleyway.

The man glanced down at Mason.

"He's my—*mine*," I heard myself declare, strangely at peace over how right the word of ownership felt on my tongue.

"Sure thing," the EMT said. "Let's get your partner to the hospital."

Partner.

The label hit me like a punch to the gut, but I didn't bother correcting the man. I believed in lust at first sight. Maybe even love for some people. Time would tell for Mason and I, but too many unknowns lay unspoken between us. We were mere strangers, and yet I felt a strong tie to his well-being. His eyes radiated emotions toward me as though hoping I would soak them up by osmosis.

And I wanted to take them on, to share in the burden of them, with a desperation I didn't understand.

My legs shook from the adrenaline crash, and I had to let go of Mason's hand when I climbed into the back of the ambulance.

Whatever else had taken place at the hotel faded from

my mind as I focused solely on the man laid out and being fussed over by the EMT. Mason struggled to answer questions, grimacing and twitching as though pain riddled his body.

I longed to wrap him up in my arms and soothe his aches. Kiss him until his discomfort faded.

My mind tucked away information as it left his lips. Thomson, he'd replied in answer to the inquiry of his last name. He was only forty-two, five-foot-eleven, and one hundred ninety pounds. He lived in the North Shore area. His health was excellent except for his current situation, and he didn't take any medications.

When asked if there was anyone else who needed to be contacted, Mason glanced at me and shook his head.

While I wasn't rich in family and friends, the fact he looked at me as though I was his person, his *only* person after we'd become aware of each other's existence a half hour earlier, made my chest ache. That desire to hold him in my arms tripled, and my fingers itched to entwine with his once more as though *he* would keep *me* on sturdy ground.

At the hospital, we were taken to a curtained-off cubicle and finally left alone a few minutes later.

I leaned over Mason, needing a closer look at his face to make sure he was really going to be okay. That sense of him being lost remained in my mind as I took in the haze over his greenish-brown eyes. Had his brain been rattled? Did he not fully understand what was going on?

"Wallet," he whispered. "Back pocket."

"You want me to get it out?"

"Yes."

Swallowing hard, I weaseled my hand beneath his lower back, chiding myself for even *thinking* about feeling up his ass that was perfectly rounded and juicy as fuck. His cell was still shoved in the first pocket I encountered. I pulled that out and went beneath his other side for his wallet. He shifted slightly with another wince, allowing me room to slip it free.

"D-Do I have any messages?"

I held his cell to his face to open the lock screen. "You've got two. One from Kellen, and one from Micah. They're both wondering if you got home alright."

"Figured they would check in," Mason murmured, his eyelids fluttering shut. "Could you answer yes then turn it off, please?"

I did as told and leaned forward to brush Mason's hair back from his forehead.

"Stay?" he murmured, his eyelids fluttering shut.

"I will," I promised, having zero intention of moving from his side unless a doctor demanded it.

An hour later, I finished filling out a few forms thanks to the wallet Mason had asked me to retrieve. I'd realized his brain hadn't been too addled by whatever had clobbered him upside the head, and he'd meant for me to take the wheel in acting as his partner.

His trust, his desire for me to look after him, intensified my yearning to get to know him better.

X-rays and an MRI confirmed he had a concussion but no internal injuries. The knife wound on his shoulder ended up being a shallow slash, only needing a few stitches. Head also sutured and bandaged, Mason finally rested, eyes closed and hand once more clinging to mine.

Luckily, he wouldn't have to be admitted overnight.

Not wanting to disturb Mason, since he'd been given some pain meds that made him loopy, I studied his face, thankful for the lack of a grimace on his full lips that appeared petal soft. My insides settled slightly over the assurance I'd been given by the nurse caring for him.

Mason had escaped his attacker intact—he would be all right.

However, with the intense emotional draw I felt toward him, I expected my heart wouldn't remain unscathed.

Chapter 3

Mason

I floated in sweet darkness. Resting. Relaxed. My mind lay quiet for a change, and I wanted to sink deeper into the sweet oblivion and forget about the shit I'd been wrestling with for weeks.

Warmth surrounded my hand, filling me with calm. Perhaps it was the firm yet soft touch that kept me cognizant.

What was it?

Who?

Blinking slowly, I attempted to rouse myself fully, even though the dreamlike state beckoning in the back of my mind promised continued peace from reality.

Blue curtains hung in front of me...murmured voices carried from beyond. Someone cried. Another person huffed with laughter. Steady beeps reached my ears, and the scent of sterility burned my nose with every inhale.

"Mason."

Turning my head awarded me a vision of the most stunning young man I had ever seen.

I stared, my fuzzy brain slowly coming back online as I

drank in the sight of his tousled dark hair and light brown eyes that studied me with the same...appreciation I felt at drinking him in.

Such a beautiful man...

"I'm Jasper, remember?" His lips lifted in a crooked smile, his petite nose crinkling slightly. He had been the one to chase my attacker away and keep me calm until help arrived.

"My savior," I added a title to his name as the memories filtered through my hazy mind.

"Hardly." He snorted a quiet laugh and squeezed my hand.

I returned the gesture, longing to be wrapped up by him sweeping over me. Tears threatened to the point I attempted to swallow the thickness from my throat.

"Are you okay?" Concern flooded his sweet voice, and his smile faded as he leaned in closer, cupping my face. "Are you in pain?"

I closed my eyes and started to shake my head on autopilot to hide myself as usual, but the slight movement made my temples ache with a dull throb. "N-not too bad," I murmured, unable to stop myself from pushing my cheek into his palm.

He smelled like the outdoors. Sunshine and the forest. Freedom.

And his simple act of gentle affection stilled the deep-rooted unrest I'd been struggling with. His was a welcomed touch, one I didn't feel the need to pull away from. For the first time, the pieces of my true self I hid inside pushed for acknowledgment. But could I trust a man I'd only just met? My heart begged yes, while my better sense, my wariness from childhood screamed no.

Being fuzzy-brained from whatever medication the

nurse had given me made the decision easy—I went with my instincts, which wanted to give the man a chance.

"You have a concussion," Jasper explained, his soft voice as soothing as his gentle stroke along my whiskers that I leaned into. "The doctor wants to keep you here for a little bit longer. Do you remember what happened?"

"Yes," I whispered, once more forcing my eyes to focus on his golden-brown irises that were as rich as amber honey. I wondered if he would taste as sweet and delicate as he looked.

"Think you could answer some questions for the cops?"

"Mmm hmm," I hummed in agreement. "Just...hold my hand?" My neediness bled through the cracks of my facade his mere presence forcibly pried open.

"Of course," Jasper agreed without hesitation, a smile making his lips go crooked again. "But I need to let them know you're awake and will have to let go for just a minute. I'll be right back. Promise."

I managed a slight nod without too much pain, sinking once more into that man-made calm as my eyes closed.

Jasper...he had told the EMT I was his. *Mine*, he'd stated then hadn't corrected the man's assumption that he was my partner.

More warmth spread through my limbs. The doc had definitely ordered me the good stuff.

I wished Jasper had kissed my forehead or shown me another form of assurance he cared. He seemed the sort that would give tirelessly—happily—the type of tender man I had only allowed myself to dream about. Ignoring under-lying wariness, I continued to float in la-la land, imagining the what-ifs with Jasper.

"Mason?"

"Hmm?" I angled my head to find he'd returned, a cop at his side towering over his slender frame.

"Detective Jenner," the man introduced himself, not bothering to offer his hand since Jasper had once more claimed mine.

Warmth spread up through my arm at Jasper's caress over my thumb.

"Could you tell me what happened tonight?" the detective asked, lifting his focus off our entwined fingers without a hint of disgust in his intense gaze.

"Yes." I swallowed, forcing my mind toward full wakefulness even though the drug-fuzz fought to creep back in. "I was at the hotel—exited out the side into the alley." The memories cleared as I spoke, my voice gaining strength and volume.

I explained how someone had followed me from the hotel but hadn't said anything and hit me before I could turn fully to see who it was. Other than a dark blur, I had no description to offer the detective.

"Another man was outside with me around the corner, and we heard Mason holler for help." Jasper took over, his thumb moving over my hand with gentle strokes that made butterflies come to life in my stomach. "I didn't get his name," he continued. "Italian-looking guy. Dark hair slicked back. He chased after Mason's attacker but didn't catch him. He returned seconds before the shooting."

"Shooting? What happened?" I asked, not remembering hearing gunshots while I'd been on the ground.

"I'm not exactly sure, but it sounded like someone fired shots in the hotel," Jasper explained.

A rush of adrenaline roused my clarity. "Where?" I asked, attempting to sit up, but Jasper pressed on my uninjured shoulder to keep me still. "The Sweet Water Suite?"

The detective shook his head. "There were gunshots, but they originated in the Westford Room. I can confirm there were no casualties, but that's all I'm able to state at this time."

Releasing a heavy exhale, I settled back on my hospital bed, attempting to cool my inner anxiety from showing. Micah and his party guests were probably safe since he'd texted me. I would have to give him and Kellen a call later and explain about the assault.

"Can you think of anyone who would want to hurt you?" Detective Jenner asked.

"No. I don't have any enemies that I'm aware of. I tend to stick to myself."

The detective had a few more questions, letting me know they would be going through video feeds—and that they'd found a knife farther up the alley. He readied to leave and told me he would like to see me down at the station the following afternoon if I was feeling up to it. He also requested the same from Jasper.

A young man in dark blue scrubs pushed aside the curtain, crossing paths with Detective Jenner as he left. "How are you feeling?" the nurse asked me, moving to my bedside.

"Okay thanks to those pain meds."

"I'm getting your discharge papers ready, but you'll need someone to be with you for at least the next twenty-four hours."

He glanced at Jasper, but I thought of Kellen, one of the few friends I trusted to be in my personal space. Unfortunately, he was heading to Maine in the morning to visit his parents. "I'm sure I'll be fine on my own," I stated with an assurance I didn't feel.

The nurse's smile appeared forced. "You really shouldn't be alone, Mr. Thomson."

"I'll stay with him."

I shifted my gaze to my right. Jasper could easily be half my age, I guessed. He had a beautiful baby face, the most lovely I'd ever seen in my life.

Jasper's sweet, crooked smile appeared again as he turned toward me. His honey-like eyes glanced over my face as though easily seeing behind the mask I'd tried to pull back into place because of the visiting nurse. "I would like to take care of you, Mason—if you'll allow it."

Why did I so badly want to trust the stranger holding my hand? Why did I feel as though fate had meant for us to meet? And why did his desire to look after me make my insides flutter and yet melt at the same time?

Jasper didn't give off hungry twink vibes, even though he appeared the type with his petite build. No—quite the opposite. He might have been twenty-something, but the young man screamed caretaker. Protector.

"Yes," I offered the answer that radiated through my core while my sense of self-preservation sank into oblivion.

I blamed the drugs.

His smile sent heat rushing through my veins, tingling life through my groin regardless of whatever meds I'd been given to help numb my nerve endings.

Looks-wise, Jasper was the boy my gay heart had been hoping to find since middle school. As for his character, his actions since my attack led me to believe he could very well be the yin to my yang.

But was he even interested in men?

That inner radar spoken of in the gay community hadn't ever worked well for me, but the way Jasper studied my face made me think he felt the connection I swore wove our spirits together regardless of my underlying apprehension.

Or maybe the painkillers I was on *were* too strong and messed with my brain's ability to function properly?

Jasper asked the nurse what he needed to do once we got to my apartment—sleep, food, medication—and I didn't bother trying to listen.

I didn't know Jasper, but all it had taken was one night in his comforting presence for him to earn what bit of trust my heart had to offer.

Hopefully, he would prove worthy.

Chapter 4

Jasper

Someone needed to take care of Mason, and not just watch over him as he recovered from his concussion. His tiny third-floor apartment forty minutes north of Boston sat in a run-down building, and I was wary of putting my feet on the filthy treads while traipsing up the stairs. With the elevator out of commission, we'd been forced to use our own energy, of which Mason had little. At least he only lived up three flights, so he hadn't been too winded by the time we'd arrived at his door. His arm draped over my narrower shoulders, easily done since he had a good six or so inches on me.

Having no clue what Mason did for work, I didn't judge the man for his shoddy furniture, but his cleanliness left a lot to be desired. Dishes stacked beside the sink. Papers sat atop his small kitchen table. Old shoes were piled in a corner by the front door.

I didn't make a ton of money working for the nonprofit LGBTQ community house in Malden, but I at least cared for my few belongings.

I took Mason into the bathroom first, gladly giving him

privacy after seeing the state of his sink and toilet. Did the man not know cleaning products existed?

While he did his business, I glanced at his bed in the apartment's only other room across the hallway. At least his sheets appeared clean, even though the comforter lay askew at the footboard.

The bathroom door squeaked, and I turned to assist Mason. He reached for my arm, grasping tightly as though afraid he would fall over without my support.

"Are you hungry?" I asked, realizing breakfast time loomed much closer than midnight.

Mason shook his head. "I would rather sleep."

"Let's get you settled." I led him into his bedroom, and he lowered to sit on the bed's edge, holding his side where he'd been kicked. While he didn't have any broken ribs, he would definitely be sore for a few days. "What do you wear to bed?"

Pink flushed his cheeks. "Um...nothing?"

Biting back a grin, I went to my knees to remove his shoes.

Do not look at his bulge. Do not look, you twit.

I managed. Barely. But I couldn't glance up at his eyes to see if he knew where my thoughts had gone.

Once I'd set his shoes and socks aside, I stood. "Need help with your shirt?"

He peered up at me like a lost puppy and nodded.

At the brush of my fingers over his clavicle while unbuttoning his dark green shirt, he sighed. I had a feeling the man would thrive from being taken care of. And my lonely heart and instincts wanted to look after him in all ways. He seemed to appreciate me. Find me worthy...

I pushed the material off his shoulders, my gaze snagging on a raw scar atop his heart. It almost looked like someone had carved a *J* into his skin. All thoughts of my childhood wounds faded at the sight of his mangled skin.

"What happened to your chest?" I asked with a frown, my voice low.

Mason turned his face away from me, his eyes closing. "Accident."

"It doesn't look like an accident."

He shrugged.

I allowed him his secrets, even though his reluctance to tell me the truth stung after what we'd been through together that night. It wasn't like I really *was* his partner and deserved to hear about what had caused such an injury. God knew I had secrets of my own I would carry to the grave.

One thing I knew for certain—whatever had caused the jagged cut couldn't have been good.

We worked together to rid his legs of his pants while I refrained from ogling the goods inside his navy boxer briefs that hugged him beautifully in all the right places.

"I'll keep these on," he murmured, rolling onto the mattress and curling up on his good side.

I dragged his comforter up to his bandaged shoulder.

"Are you really going to stick around?" Mason asked, his voice barely above a whisper, his brow slightly furrowed.

"Of course," I assured him while smoothing back his hair. "I'll be out on the couch. Just call out if you need me for anything."

"Stay with me?"

"I *am* staying."

"No." He slid his hand across the mattress between us. "Here. Beside me."

I studied his exhausted eyes, expecting the stronger

meds he'd been given in the hospital still lazed through his system. "You're inviting a stranger into your bed?"

"I'm not asking for a hookup," he stated, once more glancing away from my gaze. "Just to sleep. My couch is wicked uncomfortable."

I eyed his queen-sized mattress and how he hugged one edge. "Are you sure?"

"Yes," he didn't hesitate to answer.

Slowly releasing an exhale, I nodded.

The furrow between his eyebrows smoothed out, and he closed his eyes. "Thank you."

I turned down his blinds against the hint of the sunrise, kicked off my shoes, and laid down atop his comforter so there would be less chance of snuggling into Mason while I slept. Thankfully, I didn't work on Sundays, so I could spend the whole next day with him. But even if I'd been scheduled to go into the office, I felt sure the board I worked for would understand the situation and allow me a day off.

Being up for nearly twenty-four hours straight along with the adrenaline-filled events of the night knocked me out before I could overthink my situation.

It seemed I'd barely closed my eyes when I woke.

The clock on the bedside table told me only two hours had passed.

Mason shifted, a quiet moan pulling my focus to his side of the bed. A wince of pain lined his face again.

"No," he muttered, his entire body flinching. P-Please... don't."

"Mason." I lightly touched his good shoulder, taking care in waking him from what must be a nightmare.

"N-Not again," he begged with an anguished groan that sent pain through my chest.

"Mason," I repeated a little more firmly, needing to end his suffering.

He stilled and blinked open an eyelid. Recognition lit on his face as he slightly turned his head toward me. "Hurts," he whispered, once more clenching his eyes shut as his body relaxed into the mattress.

I hopped up and got a glass of water and the pain pills the doctor had ordered. While in the kitchen, I checked my cell I'd left on the cluttered table.

My no-show date from the night had texted his apologies an hour earlier, explaining he couldn't make it.

As if I hadn't figured that out.

I didn't bother responding. I was glad he hadn't shown up—I'd found someone with much more potential. I smiled regardless of my exhaustion, the tiny burst of adrenaline at the thought of Mason giving my feet extra pep as I walked back the hallway toward his bedroom.

Sitting on his side of the bed, I touched his forearm. "Mason?"

He moaned again, but his eyelids fluttered open.

I helped him lean up so he could take his medication and drink some water. He gingerly laid back down.

"Do you need anything else?" I asked.

"You in my bed." He sounded so serious, and I couldn't tell if he flirted or meant for me to just reclaim the spot I'd vacated. Considering he didn't smirk or reach for me, I decided he'd meant for the latter and made myself comfortable.

Mason stretched out on his back, his hand seeking out mine atop the blanket.

Our fingers entwined as though on their own accord, and I couldn't ignore the flutters in my stomach over how well we fit together.

Rather than closing my eyes, I watched Mason slip once more into a deep sleep. Full lips parted, he exhaled soft puffs of air that didn't quite count as a snore. The furrow of discomfort on his brow eased, his face taking on a more youthful appearance. Had his beard and dark hair not been shot through with gray, I would have believed him to be younger than his forty-two years.

No freckles dotted over his nose, but a few lined his shoulder closest to me. I wanted to kiss them. Map out the contours of his body hidden beneath the covers. Lay between his thighs and tell him to wrap his legs around me. Cradle me while I loved him.

Lips thinning, I closed my eyes and gave myself a stern talking-to about the swelling in my groin.

Number one, the man was injured.

Number two, I didn't know him—not really.

A year earlier, I would have been all up in his space to see if he wanted to hook up, but my desires had changed. I no longer wanted to just fuck and leave.

Number three...

There was no other reason I ought to hold back. The first two were more than enough.

Forcing myself to keep my eyes off Mason, I slipped back into rest.

ℲF
MM

The next time I woke, a blanket burrito of muscle and warmth pressed against my side, and a heavy arm slung over my chest.

Mason buried his face in my neck, his dick hard against

my thigh even though a thick comforter and my clothing separated our skin.

Lust lit through me, thickening my cock, and I lay still, my breaths shallow. Desire to turn into his embrace rolled over me like an ocean wave, tumbling my thoughts in its wake. Once more counting the reasons I shouldn't engage with him physically didn't change the yearning inside me.

I doubted anything but the satisfaction of an empty ball sac would.

No puffed exhale caressed my neck. Was Mason awake? Had he rolled in his sleep to seek out comfort? Or had he woken and done so deliberately?

"Mason?" I whispered.

A shuddered sigh rippled through him, and he shifted his hips from my body. "I'm sorry."

I slid my left hand over his forearm atop my chest, grasping onto his elbow to hold him in place. "It's okay. How are you feeling?"

"Better. But still pretty sore." His whiskers and lips grazed over my skin with every word, causing goose bumps to rise along my arms.

"I expect that'll be the case for a few days," I said, my arousal made obvious by my husky tone.

"You smell good," Mason murmured, nosing upward toward my ear, his whiskers the perfect blend of tickle and stimulating tease.

Closing my eyes, I bit back a groan. "Mason…"

"Sorry," he murmured, readying to pull away again, but I kept a tight grip on his elbow.

"Stay." Shifting my shoulders put some space between our upper bodies, and I turned my head to face him.

Mason's sleepy, greenish-brown orbs appeared more

alert than the night before, and I wondered if the narcotics I'd given him had worn off.

"What do you need?" I asked.

The black of his pupils swelled as his focus slid to my mouth.

Fuck.

I swallowed hard, knowing I ought to reword what I'd asked—water, medicine, help to the bathroom—but I didn't. Instead, I grasped his chin with my thumb and finger, tugging gently to part his lips.

"Mason?" I whispered his name, needing him to be on the same page with the one thing I would allow myself with the man I didn't want to deny anything.

Those expressive hazel eyes of his said it all. *Yes,* beyond lust—deep, intense longing.

He met me halfway, our mouths brushing gently, his whiskers soft on my face.

Tingles raced through my body clear to my toes, and I pressed in closer, my hand sliding to the back of his neck. Mason melted beneath my calming touch, whimpering in beautiful surrender to my lead. My heart soared because of it. I licked over his lower lip and slid my tongue into his mouth. He shuddered at the same time I did, the mutual desire between us more potent than I'd ever felt with another man.

The slight space between our bodies disappeared as our kiss turned hungry, gentle strokes of our tongues growing forceful. Soft noises escaped from his lungs, so needy and desperate that my dick throbbed to fill him.

He didn't make a move to take things further, and I wondered at his lack of initiative and whether it was due to his injuries or sexual preferences. While he looked like the daddy sort, he behaved the opposite, almost submissive in nature. Mason didn't go for my ass like most guys did when making out with me thinking they could get a piece of my ass.

I slid my hand beneath the blanket and grabbed a handful of his muscled backside to make my intentions clear and gauge his reaction.

Mason moaned, pressing into my hold.

My heart stuttered then thrummed three times its usual speed.

Fuck, yes.

Heavy breaths escaped between our mouths, his one hand trapped beneath my chest, the other grasping at my hair.

Shoving my palm beneath the back of his boxer briefs earned me another whimpered plea, and I slid my fingers down his crack. A deeper arch of his spine gave me all the permission I needed. Fingertip ghosting over his hole, I tore my mouth from his to watch his eyes.

He blinked, his hazel irises overshadowed by blown pupils. We stared at one another, our heightened exhales the only sound between us as I gently caressed over soft, puckered skin.

Forget not going too far and possibly causing him even more pain. Whatever Mason desired, I would gladly give him—within reason.

"What do you want, Mason?" I asked, my voice much steadier than I'd expected considering how deeply he affected me.

He swallowed hard, uncertainty filling his eyes. "Will... will you fuck me?"

Chapter 5

Mason

Jasper released a slow, steady exhale and tipped his forehead to mine. His finger continued to stroke over my hole, teasing me to the point pre-cum smeared inside my boxer briefs. I'd never been so hard without a blue pill, like a steel rod capable of knocking down a wall.

His caring for me the night before, the way he'd held me and acted as the dominant one when kissing me... His mouth had proven sweeter than I'd imagined, his generous touch seeming to stem from something deeper than the mere need to get off.

I'd been too nervous to admit what I really wanted—to be loved—so I told him what would make me feel the closest thing. I'd asked him to fuck me.

And he didn't answer.

"I need you...*please*," I whispered, desperation bleeding from the words on my lips.

Jasper shifted his head away from mine again, studying my face, his gaze full of concern. There was no calculating glint, no hardness in his stare that suggested he would manipulate my vulnerability for his own purposes. He wouldn't be a taker—I somehow knew that deep inside my bones.

Pulling his hand from beneath my boxers, Jasper gently rolled me onto my back and lifted up on an elbow to lean above me.

"I'm no doctor," he murmured, "but I'm not sure the way I want to fuck you into your mattress would be good for your head wound and bruised ribs."

"Oh, God." I gulped and grabbed the base of my dick to keep from coming in my boxers.

Jasper *wanted* to top me—and when had dirty talk become my kink?

He studied my eyes, his pupils as black as the night sky. "You would let me, wouldn't you?"

"Yes—do it," I begged.

"*Fuck*, you're a dream come true. Tell you what..." He tugged the comforter down past my hips, and I wiggled until I could kick the blanket completely off.

My dick strained upward, a large wet area darkening the front of my underwear.

"Let me take care of you, and maybe when you're feeling better, we can revisit that delicious idea, okay?"

I couldn't find words, so I simply nodded, uncaring of how my temples and side throbbed in time with my cock.

Jasper still wore his slacks and blue button-down shirt from the night before while I lay nearly naked alongside him. His hair stuck out at crazy angles, and the lack of morning scruff made him appear like a rumpled teenager.

"How old are you?" I blurted out, suddenly wary of the possibility he was *too* young.

"Thirty-three."

"Oh, shit—I thought you were like eighteen."

Snickering, he slid down the bed until his face lingered over my lower abs. "My youthful face is a blessing *and* a curse." He licked along the V that disappeared beneath my waistband, his fingers hooking to tug.

"You're beautiful." I lifted my hips, and he pulled down my boxer briefs, tossing them to the side, pink flushing his youthful cheeks at my compliment.

"Look at you," he breathed the words as though in awe of my dick he focused on. "Even if I wanted to bottom, I don't think I'd have the balls to sit on this monster."

"You only top?" I asked, beyond hopeful Jasper wasn't just a figment of my imagination.

"Mmm." He licked up the back of my length, his gaze once more on my face.

I hissed a curse, my hands cradling his smooth cheeks as he tasted me a second time. "That's a yes?" I asked, needing clarity as much as I needed his lips wrapped around my cock.

Please, please, please...

He tongued at my slit, lapping up pre-cum, his eyes growing...wary. "Yes, Mason, I only top. Will that be a problem for you?"

"Ohfuckno." I garbled the words together as he swallowed me down. "Jesus...fuck, Jasper." I trembled, fighting off the need to thrust up into his hot, wet mouth. "Want you —in my ass."

He growled around his mouthful of my dick, and I shuddered, uncaring of how needy I sounded since he seemed to like it. Grasping the backs of my knees, he pushed them up and forward, baring me fully. Jasper popped off my dick. "Okay?" he checked in, and I nodded, unable to form words. "Thank fuck, 'cuz I want to play with your hole." He shifted down, tonguing my taint, nipping with his teeth until I cursed again.

"Jasper," I whined, lifting my knees higher, past the point of caring about the ache in my ribs.

Holding my gaze, he trailed wet kisses downward until his nose grazed over my pucker. "Fuck, you smell good, Mason."

Adrenaline rushed to the point I quaked. I hadn't been touched or breached there outside of anyone but myself in years, long before I'd begun working for Elite.

Jasper settled in to feast with a low groan and slid his tongue over my crack in a slow taste. "Damn delicious."

"Jasper," I whined.

Chuckling, he licked, rimming and probing until he breached me.

I hissed a curse. "Put your dick in me before I die," I begged.

He snickered and lifted his head, fingertip swirling through the wetness his mouth had left behind. "Someone is desperate."

"Very."

"When is the last time someone stuffed your ass full with their dick, loved on your prostate with short strokes, and made you come?"

Oh, fuck, his filthy, sweet mouth.

"Years," I blurted the truth.

He blinked before his brow furrowed. His teasing fingertip stilled against my hole. "You haven't had sex in *years?*"

Shit.

I clammed up, all those rainbow-like thoughts of candor taking a hike. "I topped the last time I hooked up."

Not a lie—but far from the full truth. Jasper was the

kind of man you took home to meet your parents if you had ones who would accept the fact you were gay. He screamed wedding bells and forever.

What would he think if he knew the truth about Elite and how I earned a living?

Fuck—not the thing to consider when he was about to put his fingers up my ass.

"Please," I couldn't keep from asking again. At that moment, I would have sold my own damn soul for a taste of what I felt sure he could give me.

"I'll take care of you, Mason."

My eyes stung as he gently applied pressure with his fingertip against my spit-slickened hole. I bore down, and he slid in without resistance.

"Oh, God." I gulped against tears, eyes closing and head tipping back. I was far from full...but something other than my own fingers and silicone finally breached me. "Yes," I hissed, my dick bucking as he stroked over my prostate.

"There it is," he murmured and kissed my taint. "You like when I reach deep inside your body, don't you?" He pressed along that spot, fucking me with his finger.

"Fuck yes."

"Your hole is so needy. I love it." Nuzzling my balls, he worked another finger inside me, the gentle stretch lacking its usual sting. "So tight. God." Hot wetness surrounded one of my firming balls, and he hummed, tugging gently with his lips to keep my nuts from seizing.

My entire body trembled. Shook. I couldn't hold back the curses and pleadings for him to fuck me from spilling past my lips.

Jasper licked around my rim without breaking the rhythm of stroking into my ass, giving his fingers more wetness to work with.

I was too far gone in my need to care about the lack of lube. Cum ached to release from my balls, and I grasped at Jasper's hair, pulling him up to my dick. "Please suck me."

He sealed his lips over me, a low groan rumbling from him.

Another curse ripped from me at the tight clasp of his throat, and I thrust unintentionally.

He gagged—and took me even deeper before swallowing around my glans.

"Oh, fuck, you're going to wreck me." I lifted my head, soaking in the sight of the smears of wetness on his cheeks, the pink of his slick lips wrapped around my girth.

He opened his eyes, and our gazes caught and held. His tongue...his entire mouth moved over me, and his fingers... goddamnit, the man worked me into a frenzy. I couldn't breathe. Couldn't. Fucking. Think.

My groin tightened.

"G-Gonna come," I rasped out, every muscle in my body tensing.

He popped off my cock, saliva and pre-cum connecting us from my slit to his lower lip. "Yes, Mason—give me your load. Want it on my tongue." Jasper stroked me just right. Swallowed around me again, his throat strangling my dick.

And I came—*fuck*, how I erupted, spurts of cum gushing into his mouth. He took it all, eyes dark while he watched me unravel, his throat working to swallow what I gave him. The energy, the connection I'd felt with Jasper from the second we'd met, intensified, causing sweet agony to race through my chest.

I gasped, twitching with the last spurt and wishing he'd ingested my soul along with my spunk.

"Mmm," he hummed, tongue swirling upward along my length until he licked my glans clean. He kept his fingers buried in my ass, unmoving, the sense of fullness absolutely divine as he suckled on my slit as though wanting more of my seed. "You taste so damn good, Mason."

My hands went slack, legs splaying open. Endorphins crashed through me, making my skin buzz. "Wrecked," I murmured exactly what he'd done to me and swallowed hard while pinching myself, sure I wouldn't feel pain. I did —and I'd never enjoyed the sting so damn much.

"Did...did you just pinch yourself?" he asked.

"Yeah."

Jasper chuckled and gently removed his fingers from my ass, caressing my ring to ease the sense of loss.

The man was entirely too good to me.

And I hadn't had nearly enough.

Afraid he would roll away and leave me, I grasped at his shoulder as he wiped his fingers on my sheets. "Hold me?"

He didn't scoff at my pleading tone. Didn't make fun of me for sounding so desperate. Jasper simply scooted back up the mattress to lay beside me and tenderly wrap his arms around me. Hot exhales moved over the top of my head as I buried my face against his chest and clung to his back.

Jasper was all lean muscle and bone, and I adored how perfectly we fit together, how he rubbed along my spine with soothing gestures. But even more? I enjoyed being vulnerable with him when most people with my childhood trauma would run for the hills. Rather than questioning my lack of self-preservation, I allowed myself to enjoy him. Take what he offered without resistance.

"When was the last time someone loved you, Mason Thomson?" he murmured against my hair.

My throat swelled. I didn't need to wrack my brain to answer his question, and that settled heavily on my mind. But the fact that I was willing to *share* the truth with a near stranger regardless of how comfortable I felt with him baffled me. I hadn't ever shown those kinds of cards before.

"Never," I whispered, once more desiring honesty between us.

Jasper's hand stilled on my lower back for a few seconds before sliding once more upward toward my nape. "Mother? Father?"

I would give him what I could and pray the rest of my past would remain buried so it wouldn't be able to rock the foundation of what we'd started.

Because what we had was undeniably *something*. Something I longed to pursue. Something I wanted to last forever.

"My father was a chickenshit to his core and bowed down to my mother." I shared what even Kellen didn't know. "She was a narcissist of the worst sort, a manipulative bitch who walked all over him. I have a sister who fared about as well as I did—not too well—and we tiptoed on eggshells, knowing our father wouldn't ever stick up for us."

"My God, Mason." Jasper kissed the top of my head again while squeezing me gently as though careful of my sore ribs.

"Marin is two years younger than me," I continued, my floodgates opening. "She moved to Montana the day she turned eighteen, declaring she would never return. Six months after relocating, she fell in love with the man she ended up marrying. They've given me two nephews I've never met in person. They love me, I suppose."

I didn't tell Jasper that the younger boy was both physically and mentally challenged and that their health insurance hadn't covered all of his medical needs the previous sixteen years. Nor did I reveal that I sent my sister money every month to help them keep a roof over their heads since she wasn't able to work outside the home due to him needing care twenty-four-seven.

Yet another reason I hadn't gone to the police that night...

"What about you?" I asked while rubbing at my chest, ready to change the topic from why I'd stayed on at the job that had begun to leave me empty as a husk.

"I'm an only child. My mom adored me, but my dad was a bully of the worst sort. He always made fun of me for being too sweet, too pretty. Said I was a useless waste—" Jasper cut off abruptly, but I stayed quiet, giving him time. "He tried to beat the gay out of me when I was twelve," he eventually finished, his voice quiet and full of pain even though years had passed.

While my mom hadn't ever laid her hands on me, I hadn't escaped wound-free from my childhood. Words oftentimes hurt worse than fists.

I lay my hand over Jasper's heart, my eyes clenched shut. "I'm sorry he treated you that way, but you have to know you are *far* from useless. You're damn near perfect as far as I'm concerned."

Jasper released a quiet, sarcastic huff of laughter as though he disagreed. "You and I have different parents but similar childhood wounds. And for the record, I think you're too good to be true too, Mason."

A heavy, contented sigh sagged me thoroughly into Jasper's arms, exhaustion once more creeping over my brain.

I gloried in his hold while slipping back into sleep, praying nothing would tear us apart.

Chapter 6

Jasper

Mason released those cute puffed exhales over my chest, and I lay quiet. Contemplative.

Could the man be any better of a fit for what I'd been hoping to find? His looks, his sexual preferences, and the simple fact we shared similar upbringings, which allowed us to understand each other better than others would, *did* seem too good to be true, exactly as I'd told him.

Harsh parents had torn us both down, but while I'd risen slightly above the ashes of shit, Mason seemed stuck in his head.

Same as that deep, secret part of me I couldn't give too much mental space to still did.

Living through emotional abuse caused people to morph into hollow versions of their real self, and my heart ached to help draw him out even though I couldn't do the same for myself. I wanted to assist him in revealing the parts of his nature he probably hid from the world out of a need to protect himself.

I'd sensed Mason's floundering as he'd lain curled in on

himself because I'd becoming a nurturer at heart. Although he'd been banged up, he had also seemed lost, needing guidance and direction.

I wanted to give him both with a yearning so great my body hurt.

My dick also throbbed, but I ignored it, holding onto Mason while he rested.

Part of me felt as though we'd gone too far too fast, but hookups in my past had been in a lesser time period and without emotion. What Mason and I had shared was different on so many levels. The chemistry couldn't be beat. The easy connection, the lack of self-consciousness when our gazes held while I'd brought him release was something I'd never experienced before. I'd always been a confident lover when allowed to take control, but pleasing Mason gave me more pleasure than a climax ever would.

A few curses rang in my head, all good ones.

This is the start of something beautiful. Real. Worth the effort.

I had zero doubts—and pushed against my hidden insecurities that wanted to rise up and protest my positive outlook.

It neared two in the afternoon, and while I didn't mind my growling stomach, my head began to throb due to the lack of caffeine.

Once Mason's arms slackened around me, I weaseled my way from his light hold and crept around the dim room. My loafers sat at the foot of the bed, and I picked them up, not sure if I wanted my socked feet walking around his apartment again after that first trek to his kitchen.

The bedroom door squeaked a bit, but Mason didn't stir. I left it cracked open and slipped on my shoes since the hallway was in desperate need of a thorough vacuum.

Did Mason even have one?

I thought to look and had every intention of teaching Mason how to tidy his surroundings—but coffee called.

A quick stop in the bathroom and I took care of business, washed my hands, and attempted to tame the mess of brown locks hanging over my forehead. Mason had held on tight while I'd blown him, and the slight sting of his desperation to come down my throat twitched life back to my groin.

My nose wrinkled at the sight of Mason's old pot and the inch of cold coffee leftover from who the fuck knew when, erasing my arousal. Stains higher inside the glass pot suggested Mason didn't empty it too often—or scrub it either.

Rubbing a hand over my face, I considered the unwashed dishes and the slight smell of something nasty. Not mildew but not quite rotten food, either.

Coffee first. Then I would tackle the kitchen's mess.

Grabbing my wallet and cell off the table where I'd set them the night before, I headed toward the door—then decided to write a quick note. The last thing I needed was for Mason to wake up and think I'd abandoned him when I'd promised to stay. I had a feeling that wouldn't go over too well.

I found a pencil among the junk mail, flipped a torn envelope over, and jotted a quick explanation of where I'd gone. Creeping back into the hallway once more, I peeked in to see if he still slept.

He did.

The door didn't squeak that time, so I left it open, placed the note on the pillow I'd used, then lingered a few moments to drink in how gorgeous Mason was. My sexy, silver fox. My man to cherish—or at least I dreamed of him being mine.

God knew he needed someone like me.

Smiling, I turned away, well aware of what taking care of Mason would entail. Initially, a shit ton of cleaning products and organizational skills in which I excelled at. Having worked as the head coordinator for Humanity House for five years and overseeing the nonprofit through its expansion, I'd proven I was useful and could be trusted to get shit done.

I made sure to keep the apartment unlocked behind me so I could get back in before heading down the dark staircase. We had taken an Uber from the hospital to the hotel's parking garage after Mason's release in the early morning hours. We'd left his vehicle there and had brought mine to his apartment since the doctor suggested he not drive for a few days.

I considered climbing into my car to make the two-block trek to the Dunks on the corner but decided I could use the fresh air after being holed up in Mason's disaster.

Setting off, I wondered if his Accord was as filthy as his kitchen and bathroom.

"Ugh," I muttered to myself, not ready to even imagine its state.

I looked like a man doing the walk of shame in my wrinkled shirt, but I smoothed out the material the best I could and kept my head held high, my shoulders back regardless of how self-conscious I felt.

I soaked in the warmth of the sun, the promise of something beautiful and new on the horizon.

Dunks smelled like heaven, the hint of sweetness and toasting bagels flooding my lungs as I stepped inside the air-conditioned interior.

The line was only three deep, so I slid behind the girl at its end, eyeing the donuts in trays beyond the counter. I wondered what Mason liked. Chocolate? Something fruity? Plain? Or maybe he would prefer a muffin. Perhaps a breakfast sandwich. Deciding to order a few different items, I settled in to wait, swiping my cell to life.

No calls or new texts awaited me.

Big surprise considering I only had a handful of friends and zero plans as usual this weekend.

Someone bumped into my back.

"Shit—sorry."

I turned to find big blue eyes level with mine. Full lips with a hint of gloss made for sucking cock smiled at me. Pink flushed his high cheekbones—or rather, he'd used shimmery blush, I noted upon closer inspection. A mess of blond curls surrounded his head, making me think of an angel and a golden halo.

He took his time checking me out in return. I rarely found myself attracted to twinks, but they *had* tended to let me top in the past when I'd become bored with my hand and wanted help in getting off.

"Perhaps I'm *not* sorry," he sassed, winking once his focus returned to my eyes.

My face heated at his blatant flirting, and while I'd have done the same in return a year earlier, nothing about the young man turned me on. "Not interested," I murmured, having no wish to embarrass the kid who had a shit ton more self-confidence than I ever would.

The light in his eyes dissolved into a harsh glint.

Unease slid down my spine, and I shifted my back toward him, the hairs on my neck rousing to life. Perhaps the young man wasn't used to hearing the word no. He was beautiful enough I expected he could land whatever dick he wanted to climb aboard and ride.

But not mine.

No. I was pretty sure my body was officially off the market for the time being. Hopefully, for the indefinite future.

The person in front of me left, and I stepped up to the counter, reciting the order I'd planned in my head. Not sure how Mason took his coffee, I ordered him a large black, figuring he could doctor it up however he wanted once I got back to his place.

A brush of skin skated over my elbow, and I gritted my teeth, pretending I didn't feel that little blond getting all up in my personal space. Since when had I started giving off top vibes? Because he sure as shit would rather sit on my dick than offer me his.

Coffee tray in hand and skin crawling, I moved off to the side to wait for my food, almost queasy with the need for distance from him.

He ordered a coffee—extra cream and sugar—and headed my way the second he held his cup. "What's your name?" he asked, that calculating look still in his eyes. He wore designer clothes—fitted jeans, a pale purple crop top, and two diamond studs, a carat each at least in both lobes. The platinum color and style of his hair suggested a high-end salon rather than a barber down the street.

Considering the area of town we stood in, I wondered what he was doing there. Even worse, I had to shove down jealousy over his confidence to flaunt his femininity so blatantly.

"Jasper," I decided to answer and be honest.

"Sexy." He sipped his coffee, checking me out again. "Do you live around here?"

My brow furrowed. "No. Visiting a...friend."

"Ah." He eyed my rumpled shirt, biting on his lower lip. "A friend. From Grindr?" Laughter coated his words but sounded far from genuine—more like he fished for information I had zero interest in offering.

I forced a smile without answering and turned away, thankful as fuck that the person behind the counter called out my order.

"See you around, Jasper."

I lifted my bag his way and dipped my head in acknowledgment but didn't reply with the *I hope not* that threatened to tumble off my lips.

The kid gave me the creeps, and I could admit to myself I hated he had the freedom to flaunt his femininity, uncaring of what others thought.

I shivered while hurrying back out into the sunshiny warmth, wanting to just get back to Mason's filthy apartment. My heart rate kicked up again but in the best way. The hairs on my neck rose too, and I glanced over my shoulder, expecting the blond twink to be staring after me.

He wasn't. In fact, he seemed to have disappeared.

Turning, I hurried up the sidewalk, anxious to see where the day might potentially take us regardless of the wounds of our pasts.

Chapter 7

Mason

The scent of coffee roused me, and I filled my lungs while blinking my eyes open.

Jasper sat against my headboard, a Dunks cup in his hand. "Hey, sleeping beauty."

His sweet voice caressed me like a lover's touch, and I smiled, stretching. Popping old joints to wakefulness, my body reminded me I'd been beaten up the night before. "You left me," I teased since he smiled down at me.

"Coffee called." He shrugged and sipped, his eyes alight with happiness. "I got you one too."

"Black?" I asked, pushing up to sit beside him and taking stock of my aches. Not nearly as bad as I'd expected.

"Yes. I figured you could fix it how you wanted."

"Perfect as-is."

He retrieved the cup from the bedside table beside him and gave it to me. Our shoulders brushed, fingers grazing as he handed it over. Warmth raced through my body. Whatever trepidation or wariness that lingered deep inside me had faded.

Falling for Jasper would be too easy. Or perhaps, I'd

already tumbled head over heels. I supposed time would tell.

"Thank you."

"My pleasure." His voice flirted, and I bit the inside of my lip while checking out his mouth. "Drink your coffee, Mason," he prompted with a soft smile. "I'm not going anywhere. You're pretty much stuck with me."

"For how long?" I lifted my focus to his eyes.

"Definitely those full twenty-four hours, but I'm thinking at least until you're feeling back to normal. A couple days or a week if you need me—we'll see how things go."

My shoulders relaxed at how easily he'd taken the lead and made a plan for us rather than asking what I wanted. My *forever* answer would have sent him skittering for the hills. Sipping my coffee, I eyed the lack of morning scruff along his jawline, knowing my whiskers had to have grown an eighth of an inch while I'd slept.

"You have such beautiful skin," I said, wishing I could rub my face all over him.

"And you have a sexy as hell beard and the perfect amount of chest hair." Jasper trailed his fingertips over my fuzzy pecs, fingernail grazing my nipple.

I hissed, my focus jerking up to his amber eyes.

"Like that?" He repeated the action, which made my blood pool in my groin.

"Yeah," I rasped. "Feels good."

Jasper glanced over my chest with hungry eyes. "The things I want to do to you," he mused quietly, his hand falling to his lap.

"Yes, please."

Chuckling, he sat back once more and reached for a couple of bags on the bedside table. "I wasn't sure what you liked, so I got a bit of everything. How's your pain level?"

I considered the state of my head, shoulder, and the rest of the aches littering my body thanks to my attacker's boots. At least the fucker hadn't kicked me with enough force to cause serious damage. "Not too bad, surprisingly."

"Think over-the-counter meds will be enough, or do you want the good shit the doctor prescribed?"

I rifled through the first bag to find a strawberry jelly donut—score. "I'd rather not take any narcotics."

Jasper left me to my breakfast and retrieved some painkillers from my medicine cabinet and a glass of water.

While he was gone, I checked my phone to see Kellen had tried calling and had texted me a couple of times after I'd had Jasper turn off my cell while I'd been in the hospital.

There was no point in ruining his vacation by telling him I'd gotten jumped minutes after leaving the hotel. I replied that I was fine and would talk with him once he got home from Maine.

Jasper returned and approached my side of the bed. "If you're feeling up to it, I thought I could take you down to the police station so we can help them find your attacker. I can imagine you're ready to put this behind you sooner rather than later."

Instead of answering right away, I chewed my mouthful of sugary sweetness while accepting the pills he offered. Would closure to the case be the end of...us? Would a man being handcuffed, charged, and either fined or put behind bars make Jasper move on?

"We can do that," I stated quietly, my heart torn between wanting exactly what he said and clinging to him as long as possible. His blow job had been the best of my life. His fingers, his tongue...

I shivered at the memory, digging deeper inside for emotions I should have fought to keep buried. My past had taught me that once unearthed, my feelings could be manipulated—but Jasper hadn't shown a single hint of narcissistic tendencies.

My desire for him went far beyond lust and the intimacy we'd shared. I dealt with the crush of the century and couldn't imagine not having him in my life.

"When you're finished there, why don't you hop in the shower," he suggested. "We'll swing by my place on the way so I can do the same." Jasper squeezed my good shoulder as though sensing my need to be grounded.

His touch settled me, and I once more sank into a strongly arousing peacefulness I'd never felt with anyone. "Sounds good," I agreed, excited about seeing what the next couple of hours held.

Finally having the chance to get to know one another better without drugs or interference, Jasper and I talked nonstop on the way to his place and then the station. We had already shared the most burdensome parts of each other, the similar wounds of our childhood trauma, and chose to keep our conversation light.

Instrumental music filtered through his car's stereo, soothing and calm, a choice I couldn't have been happier with. I learned he had played the cello as a child. I loved the instrument. We laughed to find we had a shared addiction to Yo-Yo Ma and had the same exact streaming playlists as each other.

Jasper held my hand atop his thigh, fingers warm and

strong around mine. I studied how his thumb caressed the back of my hand, enjoying the electrical charges racing to my fingertips after each stroke.

"I love your hands," I murmured.

Jasper squeezed a little. "I love touching you."

Arousal rushed through my center, settling in my groin. "I can be a bit much sometimes, but with you, I'm...super needy. Maybe it's because no one has ever shown me the kind of attention you do?" My statement sounded more like a question, but it adequately summed how he made me feel.

"Perhaps you cling because you're anxious about losing something you've just found."

I lifted my focus to Jasper's profile. That soft smile curved his lips upward. How had he figured me out so quickly? "What have I found?" I asked, my voice breathless as my heart pounded.

"Potential for a close connection I think both of us want." He glanced my way, his tender gaze full of the same longing tugging on my insides.

"I'm hopeful," I murmured past the thickness in my throat, allowing him another piece of me I'd hidden away.

"Me too, Mason." Jasper lifted our clasped hands and kissed mine with a gentle brush of his lips. "Me too."

We pulled into the station's parking lot a short time later and made our way inside, hands still clasped, walking so close our shoulders bumped with every step.

"Are you holding up okay?" he asked once we sat on chairs in the lobby area while waiting for Detective Jenner.

"Just nervous. The pills helped my headache." A slow, steady inhale allowed me to calm myself so I could replace the mask I'd taken off in front of Jasper.

Keeping my hands lightly clasped in front of me, I feigned having my shit together. Held eye contact with those around us. Straightened my shoulders and lifted my chin.

The detective arrived, greeted us both by name, and motioned us to follow him. He didn't waste any time, asking if I wished to press charges if they caught my attacker—which I confidently told him I did. Detective Jenner then dove into the questions once we settled at a table across from him in a small conference-type room.

Enough space existed between Jasper's and my chair that reaching for his hand and showing my weakness would be obvious. So I didn't—but I longed to. My chest ached for his touch.

I shared about my evening from the moment I'd left the hotel, wracking my brain for every sensory memory surrounding being assaulted. While I didn't feel as though I'd given any more information than I had while at the hospital, the detective nodded, prompting me with questions from different angles. But, without having actually seen the person, I didn't have much to offer other than the strength with which they hit me and the heaviness of the boots that had battered my body.

He then went on to Jasper, listening intently and making notes as he recounted his side of the night before. Jasper stated the person hadn't been very tall—perhaps his height but was covered in dark clothing. Black jeans and boots...but a nicer shirt rather than a thug's hoodie or ripped tank top. A black ski mask had covered his head.

Unfortunately, the police hadn't been able to locate the man who'd run to my aid with Jasper.

"There are no cameras on the alleyway," Detective Jenner went on to explain. "And unfortunately, the knife we found on site only had a couple of partial fingerprints.

We're running them through the system, but it's not looking promis—"

Another man knocked and poked his head into the room. He held a file. "We got a hit."

Detective Jenner beckoned him forward, took the information, and studied it a moment. His forehead furrowed in a deep frown as he sat back in his chair. "Is this some sort of joke?"

"Both prints matched ones from those taken when he was arrested for drug possession two years ago."

Detective Jenner rubbed a hand over his shaven jaw. "Shit. Thank you, Detective."

The other man walked out, leaving the three of us in thick silence.

My pulse raced, and I struggled to keep my facade in place as I waited to hear the name of the man I couldn't wait to bring to justice. I wanted to move on with the new life ahead of me, one with the possibility of fulfillment with the sweet man beside me. He seemed the sort who would accept me regardless of my shortcomings and neediness, but the fact I worked as an escort for Elite? That truth didn't ever need to be unearthed.

I would find another job. Become a janitor and live off bread and water if it meant being able to continuing to provide for Marin's family and have Jasper's affection.

"This..." Detective Jenner shook his head, his lips thinning as he closed the file, set it on the table, and leaned forward, arms crossed atop it. "Does the name Joseph Delaney sound familiar to you?"

The blood rushed from my face. Mask ripped off, my feigned confidence was reduced to ash in a blink. Sudden ringing in my ears promised I sat on the verge of passing out.

"*The* Joseph Delaney?" Jasper asked before I could find my voice.

My attacker had been a smaller man—had slashed my shoulder with a sharp blade.

Oh fuck.

Bile attempted to choke me as Detective Jenner offered an affirmative answer.

"C-Can I see the knife?" I questioned, my voice nothing more than a ragged whisper.

He nodded and left us for a moment, saying he would be right back.

Jasper scooted his chair closer to me and gathered my hands in his, but I kept my head down, my focus on the table. My entire body trembled.

"Mason?"

I swallowed hard, shaking my head while clinging to his fingers.

Did I need a lawyer?

Could I call Micah before answering any more questions? Shit. I couldn't mention Micah, or the cops would investigate his business—or had I already used his name? I wracked my memory to see if I'd said *Micah Fox* or mentioned the fact it had been his birthday party I'd been at but came up empty.

My brain rattled as a chill settled in my bones. The door opened behind us, and adrenaline jacked through me, heating my blood where ice had frozen only seconds before. My mouth dried, and my palm grew clammy against Jasper's.

Detective Jenner sat and slid a bagged item across the table toward me.

My tumbling emotions hit a solid wall, knocking my heartbeat off rhythm. There was no mistaking the boar's head pommel with its bit of tawny leather wrapped around the handle. It had been custom-made and cost a pretty penny.

I would know—I was well acquainted with the blade that had dragged over my flesh...

Rubbing at my chest and the still-tender scar between my pecs, I closed my eyes, fighting off the vivid memory. The weight of him on my chest. His troubling, obsessive words...

Reality came in like a Mack truck, barreling through my newfound hope for something better regardless of how I attempted to leap from its path. What I had avoided for two weeks had arrived, no matter my intentions to keep the truth a secret. My past would no longer remain buried.

I imagined the rumbling thunder of the approaching shitstorm and readied myself to embrace the escape that had been engrained in me since childhood.

A complete emotional shutdown.

"You've seen this before." Detective Jenner didn't ask a question.

Stomach churning, I swallowed hard. Fear overran my body, and I clutched at Jasper's hand, sensing the false sense of peace I'd hidden behind as a kid creeping in along the edges of my mind.

Heartache instead of happiness now lay in my future.

"Yes," I whispered, sealing my fate.

Chapter 8

Jasper

Detective Jenner had to have noted the change on Mason's placid face at the mention of Joseph Delaney. But did he sense the bloodcurdling terror, the anguish, in answering he had seen the knife before?

With that one whispered word, Mason's expression once more morphed beneath my intense stare.

It was like a veil slipped over his head, hiding everything he thought, everything he felt, similar to what he had done when we'd arrived at the station but ten times as effective. He'd become a blank shell, a mask replacing his usually expressive face. Even his sweaty hold on my hand relaxed as though he'd found some inner peace when seconds before he'd clung to me as if I was a ring buoy he grasped in order to stay afloat.

Mason had big feelings. He also obviously didn't know how to process them.

I dealt with similar people at Humanity House. While I didn't have a degree in psychology, I'd spent hours with our kids and co-workers, learning all I could in order to be a better ally to those who utilized our free mental health services.

Zeke Sipe, our head counselor, had become a good friend and helped me better understand what some of the kids went through on a daily basis. Add in emotional dysregulation, a core symptom of ADHD, which a few of our kids had been diagnosed with, and we sometimes had delicate cases on our hands.

That was what I witnessed taking place inside Mason.

"Can we have a minute, Detective?" I asked, giving my attention to the man across the table.

He studied Mason with a furrowed brow, definitely aware of the flip of an emotional switch. Nodding, Detective Jenner pushed back his chair. "I'll go get us some water."

"Thank you."

Once the door shut behind him, I shifted sideways.

Mason stared at the table as though absent. Unfazed by his situation.

I wanted to *know* him, to help carry the burden of all his secrets. But would he let me? We didn't have the luxury of time on our hands, and I couldn't *make* him trust me, but I wished I could.

"Hey." I grasped his chin and turned his face toward me.

He blinked, his eyes clearing somewhat.

"There you are." I smiled and stroked his whiskers in the way I'd noticed he enjoyed. "This is all pretty upsetting, but I'm here, Mason. I'm not leaving. Focus on my hands touching you. Can you feel how much I enjoy being with you? How badly I want to take care of you?"

Mason nodded, a barely there dip of his head.

I leaned in and pressed my lips to his in a chaste kiss, lingering until his mouth softened beneath mine. "I know things are happening quickly between us, but what I feel, the draw to you, is potent. You're like the sweetest treat I can't deny myself. You're addictive. Delicious on my tongue."

More of the haunted expression in his eyes faded, and he released a shuddered sigh.

"Tell me what you need, Mason, and I'll give it to you," I pushed, recognizing the fact his thoughts had been redirected. Zeke had told me that was the number one helpful tool in the box of tricks to help someone dealing with dysregulation. "Another kiss?" I offered one before Mason answered. "A hug?" I wrapped my free arm around him, careful of the bandage on his shoulder. "Assurance of how sexy I think you are, how perfectly we seem to fit together in every way?"

He studied my eyes as though wanting to dive into my soul and hide. "You feel that too?" His unsure tone made my heart ache.

"I do," I didn't hesitate to answer. I cupped his jaw, my thumb rubbing over soft whiskers while holding his gaze. He leaned into the caress as I'd hoped for, his deep need for affection and connection tugging on my empathy. "You don't have to face this alone. I'll be here every step of the way, and if things become too much, we can leave. Seek legal counsel for direction."

His focus dropped to our clasped hands, and I allowed him a few minutes to work through whatever necessary now that he had calmed a bit and could process again. "I-I need to tell them, but I'm afraid. Ashamed..."

"You don't have to give personal details," I assured him

even though his words brought up a shit ton of questions in my head I wouldn't mind having answers to. "Stick to the facts but don't reveal anything to Detective Jenner you aren't comfortable with."

Mason sagged in his chair as though drained of energy. "I-I can do that. Then I have to make a call."

As though the detective had been listening in on our conversation—he probably had been—he knocked lightly and entered, three bottles of water in hand. He sat one each in front of us before taking his seat. Rather than asking if Mason was doing all right, he kept silent and sipped his water while we did the same.

Mason's hand shook as he set his bottle back on the table.

Our hands once more clasped together atop his thigh.

"Joseph...he and I hooked up on occasion," Mason said, his voice barely more than a whisper. Spots of color stained his cheeks. "The last time...well, he decided to introduce me to one of his kinks. Blood play."

Mason lifted the front of his shirt but wouldn't look at either of us as he did so.

The *J*.

My insides tensed, and I pressed my lips tightly together to keep quiet. I didn't shift, but all I wanted to do was find the asshole who had hurt Mason and slam my fist into his nose.

"Jesus," Detective Jenner whispered, scrubbing a hand over his jaw as he stared at the barely healed wound. "That fucking little..." He cleared his throat. "Did you, uh consent?" he asked, leaning forward onto the table, his eyes hard and yet filled with compassion.

"Yes...but not fully?" Mason shrugged, allowing his shirt

to drop back down. "I...ah, didn't press charges or anything. It had just been...for fun?"

"You're talking about Joseph Delaney the third?" the detective asked for clarity—to have it on the record.

"Yes."

I'd heard of Delaney Industries, had seen its logo pretty much every day of my life. But I didn't know anything about one of Boston's richest men and the cutting edge of technologically advanced gadgets he invented.

"And you're sure this is the knife he used to mark your chest?" Detective Jenner asked.

Mason nodded. "He bragged about it being custom-made. Makes it kind of hard to forget," he whispered, once more tightening his fingers around mine.

He spoke the truth. The end of the pommel was shaped into a boar's head, and tan leather wrapped around part of the handle. I'd never seen anything like it.

"Can you tell me how you met? Or what might have led to this latest assault?"

"I'd rather not," Mason whispered, eyes clenched shut.

"Is Mason going to need a lawyer?" I butted in, ready to take over and end his misery as quickly as possible regardless of unanswered questions. Whether it was fear or embarrassment that unsettled Mason, I didn't wish to see him overwhelmed and possibly shutting down again.

Detective Jenner frowned at me. "He's not here to answer to *any* crime—we aren't investigating him."

"Then we're free to leave." I stood, tugging on Mason's hand.

"Do you wish to press charges against Joseph Delaney, Mr. Thomson?" The detective remained seated, his focus firmly fixed on Mason's pale face.

"I-I don't know?"

Lips in a thin line, Detective Jenner nodded. "When you decide, give me a call—but don't wait too long."

Minutes later, I led Mason out to my car.

I expected him to either burst at the seams and spill everything about Joseph or either clam up. He kept silent without fully shutting down, and I once more held his hand, hoping to help keep him grounded. Concern filled me—over his silence, his slumped shoulders, the sense of...brokenness and pain radiating off him.

But if anything, I'd learned working with hurting kids that I couldn't save or heal them. Only be available in their time of need.

While I was also curious as hell about Mason and Joseph, I didn't wish to push him for information and cause even more unrest than he'd dealt with in the previous hour.

But questions burned in my mind. Suspicion leading to unease, a sixth sense I'd honed after years of dealing with my father's bullying. I tended to question people's behaviors, same as I expected Mason did due to his childhood under the care of a narcissistic mother.

I wanted to give Mason the benefit of the doubt, trust that he remained silent to hide something he merely felt ashamed of, but I barely knew the man.

"What are your thoughts on pressing charges?" I asked rather than prying into his past.

"I didn't do so then...not sure I should now." He rested against the headrest, gaze turned out the passenger window. "It all depends."

I waited, giving him a moment to expand, but Mason kept quiet.

"On?" I asked when he didn't offer further words and I couldn't stand the not knowing. How could I help him if I didn't have the facts about the entire situation between him and Joseph?

"I need to call my friend," he whispered.

And that was that.

Mason shut me out.

Chapter 9

Mason

I didn't like hiding things from Jasper, especially considering all he'd done for me since the night before, but what would he think about me being an escort? Would the fact that I fucked clients for cash sicken him? Would he turn his back on me and walk away, feeling as though he'd dirtied himself by touching me?

Such an act would devastate me. In a short time, I'd become attached to the young man holding my hand. He'd comforted me. Eased my thoughts like no one ever had.

But I needed to discuss the situation with Micah before taking a chance with Jasper. Get some direction on how to handle the legal situation. God knew that aspect would affect more people than just me if I decided to make Joseph pay for what he'd done.

"I—I'd like to be alone," I forced myself to say as Jasper pulled into my apartment building's lot.

He parked in my spot before speaking. "The doctor at the ER said you should have someone with you."

"Only for the first twenty-four hours—and that's almost up."

"That's still quite a ways away," Jasper argued with a gentle tone. He had a point. It wasn't much past dinnertime.

"I have to make a private call, Jasper." I couldn't look at his face, so I settled for staring at his hand wrapped around mine against my thigh, hoping that pushing him away wouldn't begin our ending. But what choice did I have? "There are things I need to think about. Talk through with my friend. I can't do that with you in my small space upstairs."

Jasper released a slow, steady exhale. "I'll honor your request, Mason, but you have to promise to get in touch with me if the pain gets to be too much or you need someone to be with you."

"I will." I met his gaze and tried to smile without the false face I couldn't find myself to wear in front of him. "Promise."

He studied me a few seconds while I fought off the desire to look away. I expected he could easily read the emotion in my eyes because his filled with empathy. "Okay. Do you want me to walk you up?"

If he did, I would beg him to stay. "I'll be fine," I lied yet again.

"Text me when you're in your apartment."

We'd exchanged numbers earlier on the way to the station. I'd saved him under the name Savior, which had made him scoff.

"I will." I pulled my hand from his, the sense of having a lifeline dissolving into thin air. Once more floundering in a sea of unease and anxiety, I climbed from his car. Pure stubbornness created distance between us, and every step away from his car caused an ache to radiate through my chest, deeper than the *J* Joseph had carved into my flesh. It also lowered my defenses against the jumpy anxiousness I'd experienced since the night Joseph had held me against my will.

My ears played tricks on me as I climbed the stairs, my heart racing with bursts of adrenaline. The shadows seemed to reach out to me, wanting to ensnare my wrists and ankles. Until I stood on the third floor, I felt faint, my lungs tight. Shaking hands made it difficult for me to unlock my front door, but once closed in the privacy of my home, I sagged against it.

I'm okay. It's safe here. No one can harm me.

After repeating those words a couple of times, I managed to calm my thundering heartbeat somewhat. Inhales came easier. The tremors stopped.

I texted Jasper to let him know I'd made into my apartment without issue and peeked from my window overlooking the parking lot to watch him leave. The second his car disappeared around the corner, I collapsed onto my couch and called Micah before my brain went nuts on the what-ifs.

"Mason! You missed quite a bit of excitement last night."

I huffed at Micah's greeting. "What happened?"

"There were random gunshots in the hotel's ballroom, and it caused building-wide chaos. You made it out just in time. No one was hurt though, so it's all good. I got to head home a little earlier than expected and show Jasmine my appreciation for the party she threw for me."

"Someone followed me out of the hotel and attacked me," I blurted, having no wish to think about another couple's happily ever after.

"What the hell! Are you okay?"

"Yeah, but I've got a few stitches, a nasty bruise on my temple, and a concussion."

"Shit. What happened? Please tell me the cops are working on this."

I shared the story, leaving out how Jasper and I had connected outside of caregiver and injured, and ended with recognizing the knife.

"Why do I have a feeling I'm not going to like where this is going," Micah asked, his tone low and full of concern.

"Because that blade belongs to one of your clients—and he used it on me the last night I was with him."

"Goddamnit. It's the Delaney kid, isn't it?"

"Yes," I whispered.

Micah cursed. "I fucking *knew* something wasn't right when you requested a few days off, then wouldn't take him on the other night. What went down?"

"I'd really rather not discuss it, but now I'm faced with the police questioning how I know Joseph and why he would come after me like that."

"You don't have to hide the fact you're an escort, Mason," Micah said. "How the business is set up and the contract clients sign do not mention sex in exchange for money. There is nothing incriminating on paper. The agreements include an NDA, and they sign waivers...everything is generic wording. Trust me, I made sure I could run an escort service without legal issues before starting EE. It's no different than people who join a kink club where they submit to a Dom. Lots of times there is sex involved—and the dominant parties are on the payroll."

Before hiring me, Micah had told me that while we weren't booked with the intent to have sex with clients, we were required to please them. The expectation and details remained unspoken and unwritten, but his employees didn't go in blind.

"Lying could cause problems," Micah continued. "Joseph will have proof of the transactions between him and Elite. He'll have copies of the contracts. If asked about sexual relations, you can either lie or tell them the truth. There was mutual attraction, a definite connection, that Joseph and you enjoyed each other's company and hooked up."

Not *exactly* what had gone down, but I read into what Micah suggested.

That Joseph and I had consented to sex above and beyond Elite's contract of my escorting him around town.

Micah cared about his employees and ensured we always had the option to say no. Even the paperwork signed by clients reminded them that Elite's escorts always had the right to shut shit down at any given moment if they didn't feel safe.

I should have listened to my inner voice that first night I'd been on Joseph's arm for a private dinner where he paraded me around like I was his sugar daddy. I should have taken heed of the unease eating at my stomach. And I sure as hell should have denied him my dick when he'd climbed me like a tree once behind closed doors.

The boy had been voracious, his sexual urges unquenchable. Even if I were twenty years younger, I wouldn't have been able to keep up with him. He'd become enamored with me. Obsessed. I learned that after our third "date."

I should have said no to the second one, but I was good at what I did. The cash was nothing to sneeze at, either. I'd been able to send thousands to Marin to help with their bills. No other job would have afforded me to care for her family.

"Maybe I should just sweep this whole thing under the rug," I murmured, pinching my nose in attempts to ease my growing headache.

"That's up to you," Micah said, "but I'm going on the assumption that considering the shooting mess that happened inside the hotel, the police will continue to investigate Joseph assaulting you just in case there's some connection between the two events."

"Fuck." I dropped my arm to the couch cushion beside me and tipped my head back. "What should I do?"

"You're going on vacation from work to heal, first of all. Second, you'll take as much time as you need to figure out what is going to be best for *you*. Personally, I would press charges, because what if he does this to someone else? But going after a Delaney will bring a boatload of shit to your front door. They have the money to cause a problem where there isn't really one to be found. I expect his dad will move mountains to remove any possible stain on his son's reputation regardless of his innocence or guilt. Somehow, they'll spin it to make you look like the bad guy."

I groaned at the truth Micah spoke. "I have to let this go even though I would really like to see Joseph pay for his crimes," I stated although deep down, I wouldn't be able to handle the stress. "I have to keep this a secret, otherwise Elite could be under investigation too."

"You've got to do what's best for *you*, Mason," he reiterated. "Don't worry about me or my business. I've got loopholes in place to protect me. Delaney isn't the only man in Boston with connections. It's up to you and what chances you're willing to take. But I'll warn you, the case could be big enough the media gets involved. I'll have your back no matter what you decide. My lawyers are at your disposal if you need them."

Concern remained long after I blew out a slow exhale while envisioning myself emptying my mind of worry and anxiety. While speaking with Micah had somewhat given me perspective, I wasn't sure what to do.

Withholding the truth and quitting Elite would make that part of my life a thing of the past, something no one else needed to know about. But how long would I be able to hide what I'd done from Jasper? Would it be better to tell him up front before I got in too deep?

Not even twenty-four hours into whatever had begun between Jasper and I, and I realized there was no easy answer.

I would be heartbroken either way.

Chapter 10

Jasper

I made it two blocks down the road before caving to the need to talk to someone. Dunks beckoned, so I pulled into the parking lot, put down all four of my sedan's windows, and shut off my car. Dinnertime drew near, but I figured it was still early enough I wouldn't bother my co-worker Zeke and his husband Levi by calling.

"What's up, Jasper?" Zeke answered, a smile in his voice.

"Hey. Got a few minutes?"

"Yeah. Hold on." Rustling sounded in my ear, a quiet murmur explaining he'd be back in a bit.

"How's your husband?" I asked, expecting I *had* interrupted something.

"Sunburned. We spent the day on the beach."

"You need to rub some aloe on him."

Zeke chuckled. "Already done."

"Sorry for intruding."

"We finished, otherwise I wouldn't have answered."

My face heated. Levi tended to plaster to Zeke's side

whenever he came into Humanity House. He was definitely needy but not nearly to the extent Mason was. To see their love, experience their devotion to one another from the outside would make any single gay man jealous.

I was green with envy.

"What's going on?" Zeke asked.

"Well, there's this guy."

"You hit it off with that dating app dude?"

"Shit—no. Sorry. He, uh...didn't show, but I met someone else while leaving the bar." I'd actually forgotten about the blond I'd been excited to meet that night.

"Tell me all about it," Zeke commanded, sounding settled as though he'd gotten comfortable for a long story.

So, I told him about the assault, Mason not correcting the EMT's assumption that we were partners. How calling him mine had felt right on so many levels. Caring for him. Sleeping beside him. Being blown away by the kiss of my lifetime.

"Someone has it bad."

"Yeah," I agreed while turning my car and air conditioner back on because the interior grew too hot thanks to the summer heatwave. I moved on to the whole police station scene, telling Zeke how Mason visibly escaped reality behind a thick veil of seeming indifferent.

"I used some of your redirection tools to help him refocus after the detective threw his emotions for a loop, but he pretty much shut down on me again. Not as badly as he'd done when admitting to recognizing the knife, but I knew I wouldn't get any more information out of him no matter how much I wanted it."

"How were things left between the two of you?"

I considered the lack of physical touch beyond our hand

holding, the fact he'd acted reserved and didn't seem like he'd wanted me to kiss him goodbye. "Not cold exactly, but a far cry from what we'd shared earlier this morning."

"He has a lot to process and a serious choice to make. I can't believe it would be easy considering who his attacker was. They're sure it's Delaney?"

"Fingerprints on the knife confirmed it."

"Prints aren't evidence enough these days. Who's to say they weren't planted on the stolen knife and dropped on purpose?"

It was a possibility, but Mason had been convinced the man who had assaulted him was the same one who'd carved a *J* in his skin. That last bit of information I'd kept to myself, unsure Mason would appreciate me sharing that part of his story with someone he didn't know.

Perhaps *that* was where his shame came from. That he'd allowed himself to be incapacitated and taken advantage of. How far had shit gone? Mason didn't seem the type who could be forcefully aroused...had Joseph drugged him? Raped him?

Heat flared through me. I wanted to kill the son of a bitch.

"I would give him tonight," Zeke said, breaking through my violent thoughts.

I'd been considering the best ways to dispose of a body after stabbing it to death with a boar's head pommeled blade.

"Maybe text him before bed to let him know you're thinking about him. Call him in the morning to see if he wants coffee and a donut."

I sighed until my chest almost caved in. "Thanks, Zeke. I really appreciate you answering on a Sunday night."

"Anytime. I'm here if you need me."

"Tell that lucky husband of yours I said hello," I said, my eyes stinging slightly over how perfect they were for each other.

"Will do," Zeke promised.

We hung up, but I stayed put for a few more minutes, not sure if I should return to Mason's parking lot and camp out in my car or head home which lay twenty to thirty minutes southwest depending on traffic. If he needed me, wouldn't it be better if I was only a sprint up the stairs away?

He'd asked for space, and even though I wanted to hover, I ought to honor his wishes. I had to trust Mason, after all he'd been through with his manipulative mom, that he would be able to somehow figure out how to handle his emotions toward Joseph.

But if he wanted legal advice, I knew the man for the job. I didn't have a ton of money, but I had connections. My good friend Troy Emerson worked as an associate attorney at Madden Law. His boyfriend, Silas, tended to rub elbows with the upper class—Delaney types. I wasn't aware if they spent time in the same circles though.

Might be worth looking into.

I planned to go to work the next morning unless Mason needed me, so I would give Troy a call then.

Deciding to head home, I hopped back on Route 1, and every mile extending the physical distance between me and Mason stretched my nerves thin. I didn't expect to get much sleep. Perhaps I would take a sick day on Monday, regardless of what Mason chose to do.

I heated some leftover pasta I'd made a couple of nights earlier, attempted to watch some TV, and ended up pulling my old cello out from the corner of my closet. Throat tight, I fiddled with the strings until I created a melody that didn't sound like a dying whale.

I imagined playing for Mason, or simply spending an evening together sipping wine while listening to Yo-Yo Ma playlists. Longing for both swelled so intensely I couldn't keep from reaching out.

Me: **How are you doing?**

I chewed on a fingernail while waiting for Mason to reply. Curled on the couch once more by myself, I drank a glass of wine—alone.

Mason: **Okay.**

I waited a few minutes, but he didn't send another message.

Me: **Were you able to reach your friend?**

Mason: **Yes.**

Growling at the one-word answers, my fingers flew over the screen.

Me: **I have no wish to be suffocating, but is there anything I can do to help you? I'm only a short car ride away.**

Mason: **I like that you care so much about me.**

My insides settled a bit at his openness, and my lips quirked.

Me: **I like you, Mason, and I feel strangely protective of you.**

Mason: **I like you too. Probably more than is healthy for my fragile heart.**

I yearned to beg for him to let me come back over. Spend the night. Finish up those twenty-four hours like the doctor had suggested. To fuss over him until he felt one hundred percent. Then I wanted to sink into his body and fuck him into the mattress the way we both desired.

Pressing down on my swelling cock, I sighed.

Me: **Reach out to me if you need me.**

Mason: **I think I'll need you for the rest of my life. But I'm afraid you won't stay.**

"Fuck." Boner gone, I pressed the call button.

"Hi," Mason murmured, sounding miserable as fuck.

"Thank you for sharing your feelings with me," I said, hoping he would be encouraged to continue doing so. "It means a lot to me that you trust me with what's going on right now."

"I-I haven't told you everything. I'm not sure I can."

"There's nothing you could say that will change this magnetic pull between us—I can promise you that."

He didn't reply, so I settled in to occupy his mind and help ease whatever continued to bother him over the decision he had to make about pressing charges—if he hadn't already.

But I believed he'd have shared with me straightaway if he'd set his mind on either course.

"Are you in bed?" I asked.

"Yes."

"Naked?" I added a hint of teasing to my tone.

He chuckled lightly, a beautiful sound that lightened the heaviness in my chest. "Yes."

"While I'd love to get all nasty over the phone with you, we both need some serious rest. How about you tell me a favorite memory of yours?" I suggested while closing my eyes to imagine I lay beside him rather than on my couch without extra body heat to snuggle into.

He gave me one of his. I returned in kind.

After sharing my third story about spending a weekend at Ogunquit, Maine as a teenager, I realized Mason had fallen asleep. His puffed exhales over the line made me smile. "Goodnight, precious man," I whispered. "You make my heart so happy, and I can't wait to see where this path we're on leads us."

I just hoped he allowed us a chance to walk together.

Chapter 11

Mason

I **can't stop.**

I blinked at the text from an unknown number, far from fully awake. The pinged alert had woken me up since my cell lay on the pillow beside my head. I'd fallen asleep to Jasper's soothing voice.

Rather than replying to what must be a wrong number, I rolled from bed and shuffled into the bathroom, my brain fuzzy from sleep. While emptying my bladder, I looked around the small room, actually taking note of the clutter. The filth on the mirror and faucet. When had things gotten so out of hand?

A frown dented my forehead as I realized Jasper had seen my apartment at its worst. While I'd never been super anal about keeping a clean home, I wasn't a damn pig.

My bathroom suggested otherwise.

So did the kitchen.

I had a pile of dirty dishes to wash. My coffee pot had been sitting...far too long with that inch of liquid in the bottom. Grimacing, I glanced around, realizing too many plates and bowls filled the sink to make cleanup easy. The countertops were a mess as well, leaving no room to shuffle dirty shit from the sink so I could even run the damn water and wash them.

Tension coiled in my stomach, the onset of crippling anxiety. I was going to shut down...

I spun on my heel and collapsed onto the couch, gently cradling my pounding head in my hands.

Coffee. A walk.

I needed to focus on putting one foot in front of the other.

My disaster of an apartment could wait.

Laundry spilled from my basket—clean clothes, thank goodness. At least I'd managed to accomplish that chore before the weekend had hit and thrown me for another loop.

I tugged on some gym shorts, a wrinkled T, mismatched socks, and the new sneakers I'd bought for myself at the beginning of the summer. My single splurge since I'd begun making good money at Elite.

Shoving aside those thoughts too, I descended the building's stairs without the same jumpiness as the night before and smiled at the warmth of the sun shining on my face. At least it didn't rain.

Dunks called out my name, and focusing on the orange and brown of their sign, I traipsed forward without a lick of my usual anxiety. A few minutes later, I held a tall, black coffee, the steam rising to tease my nose. Dark, bitter brew slid over my tongue, warming me straight through to my empty stomach.

I meandered back outside, not yet ready to return to my dingy apartment since I'd somehow managed to keep perpetual worry from taking over my mind. My home was far from the best place, and I could have definitely afforded better, but Marin's family's needs outweighed my own. Someday soon, I would buy myself a plane ticket and visit her and the boys in Montana. I'd always loved the outdoors, the wide open spaces.

Maybe I could move there.

That would mean leaving Jasper behind.

My stomach churned at the thought. I barely knew the man, but he'd become…an integral part of my life. A steady exhale to rid my mind of being without him, and I sipped my coffee, deciding I would stay put. Jasper had told me he worked at Humanity House, a community home for LGBTQ people in need. Talk about a fitting job—a rewarding one. I wouldn't ever ask him to leave a job that was ten times more worthy of accolades than getting paid to stick your dick in greedy holes.

I wasn't ashamed of how I'd earned money the previous six months, so why did the idea of Jasper finding out cause me to swallow rising bile? I tossed my coffee in the nearest trash and headed toward my apartment building, my good mood and calm state ruined.

Jasper was a kind soul, gentle and loving, but who would want a relationship with someone who'd fucked hundreds of times outside of connection and true intimacy?

Perhaps I *was* ashamed—

A dinged alert made me pull my cell from my shorts' pocket.

Unknown Number: **You broke my heart by denying me. Don't fool yourself into believing I'm done with you yet.**

Hair follicles roused over my nape and arms, raising goose bumps along my skin. Adrenaline shot through my system, causing me to shake.

Me: **Who is this?**

Unknown Number: **Your blond angel.**

Fuck.

I bent over and puked, coffee and bile spewing across the sidewalk. Two teens approaching from the opposite way cursed, jumping aside, but neither thought to stop and ask me if I was okay. Not one person around checked in with me as I gagged and spat.

Stumbling forward, I hurried home, wetness rolling down my cheeks. I'd called Joseph *blond angel* that first night together because he loved having a pet name, and those cute curls had made me think of a cherub.

The young man was far from pure and innocent. A celestial being, he most definitely was not. He'd been spawned in the pits of hell and deserved to burn in fire and brimstone for all of eternity.

I managed to climb the stairs again without losing my shit. I locked myself in my apartment, shut off my cell, and crawled into bed, a pillow over my head. Even though I'd been tempted throughout life to drink my worries away, pop a few extra pills that would chase off overwhelming emotions, I had never crossed that line.

But while lying there all alone, sick with worry about when Joseph would come after me again, how pressing charges would possibly hurt more than just myself, I lusted for oblivion.

My prescription...

I dragged my ass out of bed. The bottle sat on the kitchen table with a pile of papers I couldn't remember tossing there.

Tears tracked down my face, dripping onto the bills I needed to pay. I hadn't been able to find the energy to take care of them since Joseph had used his knife on me weeks earlier. He'd gotten his money's worth out of me that night. Whatever he'd slipped into my drink when I'd first gotten to his condo had made my dick as hard as granite and my inhibitions like a flimsy paper plate.

But had I not agreed to sell my body for sex, I never would have experienced that horror. I had no one to blame but myself.

Swallowing a sob, I emptied the bottle into my palm.

Ten pills.

The memory of Jasper's crooked smile and tender amber eyes flitted through my mind, making my chest ache. I thought of the last time I'd video chatted with Marin and her boys. They'd gone on a weekend camping trip thanks to an extra two hundred I'd wired to my sister. It had been their first family vacation. The boys had learned how to fish, and they'd cooked marshmallows over an open fire. Being able to provide that for them, seeing their shining eyes and words of thanks—they would be devastated if I chose selfishness.

Sniffing, I funneled my palm and slid eight pills back where they belonged. The other two, I popped between my lips and swallowed down with a few sips of water straight from the faucet.

The dirty dishes beneath my nose fucking stank to high heaven.

But I had nothing left. I needed to rest. Disappear from reality for just a little while.

My extra pillow comforted my throbbing head, and I burrowed my face in the traces of Jasper's woodsy scent, seeking out the emotional freedom I'd enjoyed with him. He would have held me. He would have helped me.

Maybe he would love me.

Fuzziness wavered along the edges of my consciousness,

and I finally settled into deeper relaxation than I could force on myself. I sank into darkness where nothing mattered anymore.

Peace and quiet surrounded me. I felt no fear. No pain. No anxiety or worry...

A loud pounding woke me, and I blinked myself to semi-wakefulness.

A muffled shout reached my ears.

I rubbed my eyes while rolling onto my back, my head reeling.

"Mason!"

I barely made out the voice calling atop the fists on my door.

Jasper.

My pulse sped, but I struggled to drag my numbed ass from bed and stumble down the hallway. The knock came again, and I fumbled to unlock my door and pull it open.

"Oh thank fuck. Mason." Jasper threw his arms around me, squeezing me tight. "I was so worried—you didn't answer my texts, and your cell went straight to voice mail. Are you okay?"

"Was sleeping," I slurred, still out of it from the pills that had allowed me some undisturbed rest.

Jasper stepped back and grabbed hold of my cheeks, studying my face. "Are you drunk?"

"Nah—pills. The good kind."

"How many did you take?"

"Two."

"The dosage is one." His lips thinned, his disappointment clear and making me want to shift beneath his scrutiny. He shut my door behind him, locking us in. Once he turned to face me again, his propped his fists on his hips.

"Were you in pain or just needing to disappear for a little while?"

I didn't answer right away.

"Mason."

I blinked, bringing my focus to his eyes. He wasn't angry...just concerned.

"I-I'm feeling overwhelmed," I whispered, fighting off the thoughts that wanted to crowd my mind. "It's crazy, but you're the only thing—person—who makes my head quiet. I-I shouldn't have told you to go."

"Come here, Mase." Jasper grasped my hand and led me back the hallway to my bedroom. "Strip down and climb under the covers. I'm going to hold you until you sleep off those narcotics."

"You called me Mase," I murmured while he helped me out of my shirt.

"I hope to someday call you sweetheart. Baby. My lover."

"Yes, yes, and yes," I said, sounding loopy as fuck. I thought I grinned.

"What am I going to do with you?" Jasper murmured while dropping to his knees to remove my sneakers I'd never kicked off when I'd gotten back from Dunks.

"Keep me."

His amber eyes lifted to focus on my face. "I think I want to—no, I *know* I do."

"I feel the same."

He stood, leaned in, and kissed me sweetly on the lips. "Shorts—then get under those covers, baby."

I hummed my happiness over the pet name and shoved at my shorts until they caught around my ankles. I swore I had four thumbs.

"Fuck, what a sight," Jasper murmured, widening my grin as I lay on the bed, legs hanging off the side.

"I've got a big dick, but I hate topping," I muttered.

Jasper chuckled. "What other truths do you want to share with me while you're high as a kite?"

"I could love you." The words fell from my lips since my subconscious held the reins. But I didn't care in that moment.

Jasper paused from folding the shorts I'd kicked free.

I fought to focus on him as he slowly continued before setting them atop my bureau. Standing between my legs, he peered down at me. "I could love you too, Mason. Easily. I want to *make* love to you like you wouldn't believe, but there will be time for that later."

My heart should have gone pitter-patter, but the pills brought about a numbness that didn't allow full emotional responses.

Sighing, I allowed Jasper to help me get beneath my rumpled comforter where I sprawled on my back. "Get naked. Want you with me," I murmured, a hovering sense of fear he would leave attempting to break through the drug haze in my brain.

Jasper didn't argue, simply removed his clothing—T-shirt, khaki shorts, and white briefs.

"You're beautiful," I murmured as he crawled onto my bed, his thick cock making me wish I hadn't taken those damn pills. I longed to feel his perfect girth stretching me, every inch of him buried deep inside my body.

"You can't look at me like that right now." Jasper planked over me on hands and knees.

He was so damn hot above me like that—wanted him to stay there for-fucking-ever. I grinned, the heaviness in my chest easing from his close proximity. "Can't help it."

Jasper flashed a crooked smirk that made me want to bite his full, lower lip. "It's a good thing I'm so much younger than you, old man," he teased, leaning down to brush his mouth over mine with too quick of a smooch. "Because I have a feeling you're going to be insatiable once you're sober."

"Mmm," I hummed an agreement, snuggling in against his side when he finally stretched out beside me.

He tucked my face against his neck, his hand cradling the back of my head. "Rest, baby." Soft kisses brushed over my hair. "I'll hold you while you sleep."

I passed the fuck out.

Chapter 12

Jasper

Mason slept like the dead, and I eventually grew too antsy to lay still.

I slid on my pants, attacked the dirty dishes, then moved on to the kitchen table's paperwork—trash, more like it. A few bills appeared to be unpaid, so I left those alone, getting rid of the junk mail and any other piece of paper that didn't look important.

His cell sat atop the table—turned off, which explained why he hadn't answered either my texts or calls.

I found an old vacuum in the hallway closet but didn't want to wake Mason so set that task aside for later. I scrubbed out the coffeepot then made fresh instead.

Back in my briefs, I leaned against Mason's headboard with a cup of steaming joe. Minutes later, Mason finally stirred, slowly blinking open his eyes. He caught sight of me and gently rolled into my legs with only a slight wince, slung his arm over them, and rested his cheek on my thigh.

His mouth lay too damn close to my cock.

My fingers found his hair on instinct, and I scratched at

his scalp, taking care to avoid his stitches. His low moan twitched life through my groin. "Sleep well?"

"Mmm," he hummed an agreement. "I don't think I'm high anymore."

"Can I get you some coffee?"

"Want to stay just like this until I wake up a bit." He sighed, snuggling in closer and nuzzling my bare thigh with his soft whiskers.

I didn't bother chastising or stopping him. If he felt better, I wasn't about to say no to whatever he begged for. Probably my dick. Blood seeped into my length, but I ignored it, sipping my coffee and playing with Mason's hair.

"I really want to fuck around with you," Mason finally said, his voice still sleepy, "but I have dragon breath, I need to shower, and I'm starved since I haven't eaten a damn thing all day."

Chuckling, I set my coffee aside and climbed from the bed. "Then get a move on, my soon-to-be lover."

"Jesus." Mason rolled onto his back, giving me an eyeful of his impressive cock at half-mast. I couldn't imagine sitting on that monster...

He'd topped last time he'd had sex—with Joseph.

My stomach curdled the coffee I'd swallowed, and I grabbed up my pants and turned away, annoyed at my jealousy. He was no more a virgin than I was. I had no right to be upset about past sex partners.

"I'm sorry about the state of my apartment," he murmured as I quickly dressed.

I paused from leaving the bedroom to glance back at Mason.

"I'm not usually this much of a pig—I've just been off-kilter since that night with... Anyway, I shut down to pretty much everything except surviving the past couple of weeks.

I tend to lose my sense of priority when I get overwhelmed, which is quite often if I'm being honest."

A smile quirked my lips. "I understand, Mason. And thank you for sharing that with me. At least you recognize what happens. That's something we can work with."

Mason sat on the edge of the bed, eyeing me. "What do you mean?"

"I'm going to create a chart for you. A few chores every day will help make things easier and keep shit from piling up until you're out of this funk."

Wetness welled in his eyes. "I'm a loser."

"The fuck you are." Frowning, I returned and dropped to my knees between his legs. I grasped his cheeks. "You just have big feelings, emotions you've never learned how to process. But that can change, Mason. I'm going to help you, and you're going to let me."

He sagged into my hold, nodding as though happy someone else took the reins.

I tipped his head and kissed his forehead, since he'd claimed to have dragon breath. "Shower. I'll go get you something to eat."

Fifteen minutes later, he joined me in the kitchen dressed only in boxer briefs, his hair still damp and droplets of water clinging to his chest hair around that damned *J*. Regardless of that scar and how he'd gotten it, Mason was a tall drink of water I was more than ready to swallow down. But, the man needed food in his stomach more than my dick up his ass.

He glanced around the kitchen while settling into a chair at his semi-cleared table. "You didn't have to do all this."

"You're right," I agreed while slicing the last too-ripe strawberry he'd had in his fridge atop the waffle I'd made.

The iron had sat atop the countertop and appeared well-used. He also had two boxes of dry batter mix in the cabinet above it. "But I cleaned up to lessen how overwhelming it probably seemed to you."

"It was. Thank you."

I set the plate in front of him and used spray whipped cream to top his breakfast off.

"You made me waffles exactly how I like them." His voice broke, and he swallowed hard.

Smiling, I kissed the crown of his head and rummaged in the bag the ER nurse had sent home with us. "Dig in, baby."

While he ate, I taped smaller bandages to his temple stitches and shoulder. "How are you feeling?"

"Much better." He chewed slowly, glancing at his cell phone with wary eyes.

"What's wrong?" I asked, sitting down beside him.

"Just...texts. It's okay." He busied himself with his last bite of breakfast.

He needed help, someone else to lead—so I did.

I set aside the hospital bag and picked up his cell to power it on.

"Jasper," he whispered, but I shushed him.

The lock screen revealed a dozen messages, so I swiped. Other than the few I'd sent, they were all from the same unknown number throughout the day. But, it didn't take a genius to know who'd written them. Each one was worse than the last—outright threats to give him another chance or Mason would pay. Reminders of how good they had been together, how much Joseph had loved bouncing on Mason's dick.

I wanted to puke.

You're being cruel! Answer me!

Text back or you'll be sorry!

I should have stabbed you in the fucking throat!

"You can't just let this go, Mason." I powered his cell back off without replying, glancing up to find him studying his plate. "You have nothing to be ashamed of. This is not your fault. The kid is obviously disturbed."

"I-I just want it to go away," Mason muttered.

I rubbed his back as his shoulders sagged. "When you're done eating, we're going over to my friend Troy's house. He's a lawyer. Maybe he can offer us some direction on what you can do to make him stop."

"Can I have your dick first?" Mason asked with a suggestive tone, a slight smile curving his lips. He definitely felt better—and had a mischievous, bratty side.

I liked it.

"After," I promised. "With this shit on my mind, I don't think I could keep it up and give you the dicking you've gone too long without."

His pupils swelled, cheeks staining red as he stared at me with that hungry look I struggled to deny.

"Nuh uh." I stood and took his empty plate to the sink before he got the best of my good intentions. "Attorney, then dick."

JF
_{MM}

I called Troy while Mason covered his delicious nakedness. My friend said he was free for us to come over and that Silas was still at the office and wouldn't be home until later.

We hit some rush hour traffic on the way to their condo in Boston. I'd been to their place a couple of times, but the entire wall made of up windows overlooking downtown always blew me away. Their home was an open concept layout, high-end appliances in a chef's kitchen I would have died to spend hours in.

Same as when we'd gone to the police station, Mason hid behind his public mask, but I had expected it.

Troy offered us both a martini, which we graciously accepted and sat in the living area. Fading sunlight glinted over the State House's golden dome in the distance, highlighting Troy's angelic appearance. He was fair to my dark, with pale blue eyes and strawberry-blond hair that had grown longer since I'd seen him last. Also unlike me, he felt free to experiment with his feminine side, oftentimes wearing softer colors I envied and gloss I'd seen Silas lick off Troy's lips more than once.

But Silas Barlowe was one of a kind. Nothing fazed him, nor did he care what people thought.

I'd expected Mason to put space between us like he'd done when Detective Jenner had questioned us, but he sat beside me on the couch, his shoulder and knee touching mine, reminding me of his insecurity and need for direction.

Mason was nothing like Silas, and although I longed for complete freedom to be myself, I wouldn't trade him for anything under the sun. We fit in all the other ways that mattered.

"Jasper told me you're having problems with a stalker," Troy said.

"Yes." Mason clutched his martini glass, not having taken a single sip.

"Can you tell me about him?"

Mason glanced at me, the first break in his façade, and I nodded. While I could have shared all I knew, Mason ought to speak for himself. I placed my left hand on his thigh, since he seemed to need moral support. "Go ahead, baby."

He filled his lungs then spilled the brief story about his dates with Joseph that led to the attack outside the hotel. I'd expected more details, but Mason kept those to himself, exactly as I'd told him to do before speaking with the detective. I hoped to one day hear everything that had gone down that night but only when he was ready. Pushing for more might set him back, and I wanted him comfortable more than anything.

Troy studied him for a few minutes after Mason finished, his gaze assessing. Calculating. "Are you planning on pressing charges?"

A slight shrug shifted Mason's shoulder against mine. "I would really rather not...I just don't have the mental capacity to see something like that through to the end."

His candid response surprised me.

"What about a restraining order?" I asked Troy, hoping to give Mason a little respite.

My friend finished his martini and set it aside. "A 209A order requires a family or household member or serious dating relationship, of which three dates wouldn't count. A harassment order, however, fits this circumstance."

"What's that?" I asked.

"A harassment order would require this person stay away from and have no contact with Mason for up to a year."

"Is that our only option?" I questioned when Mason remained silent.

"Outside of pressing charges, yes," Troy replied.

"It's...much too complicated," Mason murmured, giving Troy his full focus.

"Can I ask why?" he asked.

"Because of who he is?" It sounded as though Mason had more to say even atop that truth but wasn't sure if he should.

Troy waited, one eyebrow raised with a look that probably made people on the witness stand blurt the truth.

Mason cleared his throat, shifting on the couch, but surprisingly held Troy's gaze. "Joseph Delaney."

Troy's face didn't twitch at the name. "I'm assuming you mean the third? Blond, innocent-looking boy who is also a spoiled-rotten punk?"

"You know him?"

Troy dipped his head. "Our office defended him a couple of years ago—drug possession. I told my boss Noah I would never take a case for a Delaney again."

The front door unlocked before I could question why, and the three of us turned our heads. Silas strode in dressed in a full suit and tie—of the finest quality, like everything else in his condo. Whenever Silas entered a room, his presence commanded attention and rippled with a sense of power that would intimidate even the most stoic of men.

His focus landed on Troy first, the intense furrow between his eyes smoothing, hazel eyes going from dark and broody to light and carefree in an instant. I'd seen his expression morph countless times when laying his eyes on his partner.

Silas dropped his bag on the table and went straight to Troy, leaning down, hands on the chair's arms. Pink flushed Troy's cheeks as he peered up at his lover.

"How's my elfin angel today?" Silas murmured before kissing Troy's lips. They lingered briefly, just long enough that I grew antsy. It was sickening, really, how they couldn't keep their hands off each other, but I was happy for my friend.

"I'm better now that you're home," Troy said, tugging on Silas's tie to hold his face close. They shared another kiss, and Silas eventually stood, turning toward us.

"Jasper." He rounded the coffee table and shook my hand, his grip powerful as always. "Good to see you again."

"Silas," I said, resting my palm on Mason's thigh. "This is Mason." I hadn't been sure what label to give him since he was more than just my friend. Lover? My future?

I looked forward to the first and hoped for the second.

"Mason," Silas greeted him, and they too shook, Mason's cool, indifferent demeanor back in place. Being able to hold that with Silas? Mason was a damn rock star with nerves of steel when required. He definitely had another side to him I hadn't yet met. But we had time. I had plans—to know the man inside and out. Especially his desires and dreams, so I could help make them come to fruition.

Silas stated he needed a drink and strode into the kitchen. "Need another one, boy?" he called out.

"Yes, please and thank you," Troy told him. He glanced at our glasses we'd barely sipped from. "Would you like to stay for dinner? It's my night to cook tonight, so I'm ordering Thai."

Silas chuckled.

"What?" Troy asked, casting a glance at his partner in the kitchen. "I was in court all day and don't have the energy to spend an hour slaving in the kitchen."

Silas joined us once more and set his tumbler of clear liquor over ice and a second martini for Troy atop the end table. He tugged Troy off the chair, settled in the vacated seat, and pulled him down atop him.

A soft laugh escaped Troy as he sprawled sideways over Silas's lap. "Much better."

"Mmm," Silas agreed and retrieved their drinks. "So, Mason, you've gotten yourself a good man." His gaze flicked to my hand on Mason's leg.

"Yes," Mason didn't hesitate to agree.

Warmth flooded my cheeks. Had he just claimed ownership of me?

As Troy had stated, *Yes, please and thank you.*

Chapter 13

Mason

Jasper seemed pleased by my simple reply, his fingers squeezing my leg.

I set aside the martini that smelled much too strong for my liking and slid my palm beneath his so our fingers could tangle. I'd been hesitant to reveal too many cards in front of strangers, mainly my need for Jasper, but with how Silas and Troy clung to each other, I didn't fear judgment.

Talk about a power couple. They were intimidating as fuck and yet sweet as maple syrup together.

Oh, to have that kind of love.

"And what do you do for work, Mason?" Silas asked before sipping his drink.

My heart stuttered, and I swallowed down rising panic that attempted to fracture my false front. People like Silas and Troy, the upper crust so to speak, would certainly be snobbish enough to consider how I supported Marin a disgrace. "I...um, I'm between jobs right now."

Not exactly a lie since I didn't see myself going back to Elite unless Jasper dumped me sometime soon.

"What sort of skills do you have? Degrees?"

Straightening my shoulders, I fixed my mask firmly in place. "I managed to get two years of schooling in—I was going for business, but then I had to move out of my parents' home and couldn't afford to pay for everything on my own. After that, I worked wherever I found a place in need. Ten years ago, I landed a job with Carter Communications in the sales department. It was steady, decent pay, and I enjoyed utilizing some of what I'd learned in college."

"Carter went under in December of last year," Silas said.

"Yes." I left it at that, not about to explain how my friend Kellen had introduced me to Micah shortly afterward.

"I tried to buy them out before they folded." Silas's lips thinned as he shook his head.

Jasper had told me that Silas acquired flagging businesses, utilized the team he personally trained that helped build them back up, then he sold them for profit. I'd expected him to be rich, but Silas was...much wealthier than anyone I'd met. Joseph Delaney included.

"I offered them way more than they were worth," Silas continued, "but the owner's goddamn stubbornness... I'm sorry you lost your job, Mason. So what have you been doing since then?"

"A little of this and that." I shrugged, hating how I lied and my stomach clenched because of it. "My savings has been seeing me through."

"We always have job openings, and in fact, we're in the process of putting a second team together. Pop online later and see if anything feels like a good fit for you. Even if it's something lower down on the pay scale or not exactly your wheelhouse, get your foot in the door. I'm all about tutoring hard workers in how I conduct business and watching them rise in the ranks."

Silas Barlowe didn't even know me but trusted me because of the man I sat beside.

Gratitude welled up inside me, and I struggled to fight off tears. The last thing I wanted was for the powerful, ridiculously masculine man to see me as delicate pansy like my dad had been and I tried not to be.

"I will. Thank you." I barely held myself together emotionally, but at least my voice didn't waver.

Jasper squeezed my hand and turned the topic elsewhere, taking the spotlight off me.

He *did* know my mind. Had to with how in tune he seemed with my feelings.

We spent the next two hours with Silas and his lover, and while I felt a little out of my element, I'd been in the presence of all sorts of people in my time with Elite. Having the Joseph situation settled somewhat in my brain for the moment, I was able to focus on playing my part. I donned the persona I'd learned to wear thanks to my mom, hiding most of the real me in my back pocket. That was the Mason Elite clients had known: a somewhat polished middle-aged man with enough confidence and knowledge to put people at ease and carry on a conversation.

Silas and Troy seemed to like me well enough—not that they tore their eyes off one another often or for very long. Their love, the connection they shared, made me desire the same with an intense ache.

Jasper and I had a foundation to build upon, our mutual desire for unbeatable. We just needed more. Dates. Hours of pillow talk. Time spent learning one another's bodies. All of which I hoped for and feared not being able to have.

"Will you come home with me?" Jasper asked once we'd

bid goodnight to Silas and Troy and shut ourselves in his car.

"I'd love to."

He flashed a crooked grin that warmed my insides and sent blood rushing to my groin. "Is your head feeling okay?"

I touched the still-tender bump near my temple covered with a smaller bandage. "Yes."

"Shoulder?"

"I'm good, Jasper. More than well enough for you to fuck me into the mattress like you promised."

He hissed a curse, pressing down on his dick. "You're going to make me break the speed limit."

I laughed and reached over to grasp his upper thigh. "Take your time," I murmured, sliding upward to cup his bulge, his cock thickening against my palm. "I'd rather my balls ache and arrive safely than end up in the hospital again because you drove into a ditch."

Jasper grabbed my wrist to stop me from stroking him. "I think you need to sit over there, keep your hands to yourself, and let me concentrate on getting us to my bed in one piece."

I did as told, smiling. "I like it when you're bossy."

"I've noticed." Jasper shot me another grin. "And I love that you appreciate who I am and how I want to love on you."

"Have you *ever* bottomed?"

"Once, and I hated it. And before you say that the guy must have gone about it all wrong, that I would have enjoyed it if it had been done right—I dated him for a year before I gave in. There was something like love between us, and the chemistry was far from lacking." Jasper shrugged. "It's just not for me."

"That's how I feel about topping."

"There are no expectations here, Mason," Jasper said, his voice growing serious. "It's easy to assume that we'll be a perfect match in bed, but if we're not, that's alright. I want you comfortable, for you to experience nothing but pleasure. Safety."

"You're one of the few people I *do* feel safe with," I told him, wishing I didn't have to clasp my hands in my lap like a little kid when I wanted—needed—to have physical contact with him. "For some reason, I'm not able to squash my emotions when we're together, and strangely, I'm perfectly okay with that." I glanced at him out of the corner of my eye, somewhat emboldened by the jealousy I'd felt over his friend's relationship. My heart rate sped up from a slight adrenaline release. "I have high hopes for us. I think this is the beginning of something beautiful."

His eyes darkened when he glanced at me, promising the same sentiment.

But he didn't speak the words I'd longed to hear.

Heaviness threatened to sink over my mind, but I couldn't dismiss the way Jasper looked at me. What his touch conveyed every time his fingertips brushed over my skin, how his hand always reached for mine and clung with the exact same desperation I experienced when around him.

My hands tightened together atop my lap, and I struggled with wanting to reach for him and being good so as to not distract his driving.

When we arrived at his building, he opened my door and offered me what I'd been needing. My breath left in a rush as our fingers tangled once more, easing my insecurity that maybe we *weren't* on the same page. Legs shaking, I followed him into his house in Malden, mere minutes from Humanity House where he worked.

Unlike Troy and Silas's place, Jasper's didn't have a million-dollar view, fancy artwork on his walls, or a state-of-the-art kitchen. But he did have a home, one that I'd learned the day before while stopping by on the way to the police station was comfortable with bright pillows and a fleece throw on the couch. There were even a couple of watercolors and pencil sketches stuck on his fridge—kids from Humanity House, he'd explained.

"It's not much," he said, same as he had the first time I'd followed him in, while tossing his keys onto his island/eat-in bar in the middle of his kitchen.

"It's clean and comfortable," I reminded him and kicked off my shoes, appreciating the scent of freshness. No dirty dishes littered his sink or Formica countertops.

Pink blushed Jasper's cheeks as he took my hand and led me into his bedroom. "You just showered a little while ago, but if you need—"

"I prepped at home."

He smiled and tugged me into his arms. "You're wonderful."

"I'm not."

A huffed snort escaped him. "You *are*, Mason Thomson, and I won't hear any different from your lips, understand?"

I nodded, ready to melt into him and lose myself to the pleasure I yearned for.

Jasper leaned up a couple inches to reach my mouth, his lips hovering over mine. "I have a secret...I *know* what we have is something beautiful like you suggested in the car on the way here. I feel it deep inside my heart. My soul. But I didn't wish to speak of it without being able to consume you immediately afterward."

Intense longing shot through me. I whimpered, clutching at his shirt.

Jasper pressed his lips to mine, and same as our first kiss, weakness slid through my limbs. The gentle touch of his mouth, the slick glide of his tongue along my seam asking for entrance, made me want to fall to my knees, spread my ass cheeks, and beg him to fill me already.

The sweet kiss turned greedy, and rather than submitting, my hunger met him lash for lash, nip for nip, both of us breathing heavily and clutching at one another.

"Please don't make me wait," I begged after tearing my mouth from his. My cock throbbed for release, and I feared erupting the second he sank his dick into my ass.

Jasper began to undress me, and I stood still, allowing both of our desires to be fulfilled. His to care, mine to finally be on the receiving end. He removed my shirt first, standing behind me to check my bandage. His tenderness caused my eyes to sting and chest ache.

"I love these freckles," he murmured and kissed his way across my shoulder blade. "And this back..." Jasper slid his hands downward to the swell of my ass. "You're so damn sexy, Mason." Pressing against me, he reached around and worked open my jeans, tucking his hands in to shove them downward.

I fisted my hands at my sides, head tipped back and eyes closed as Jasper brought my dreams to life. No one had ever worshiped me like he did, kissing the base of my spine, each of my ass cheeks while sliding my jeans and boxer briefs to the floor. He made me feel like a god. Important. Wholly accepted, every inch of me appreciated.

His hot breath ghosted over my backside as his hands swept up over my calves to the backs of my knees, up my thighs to my ass. His thumbs swiped through my crack, and I shuddered as he spread me. "Fuck, Mason." He swallowed audibly.

He nosed over my hole, inhaling. "Smells so good."

"Shit," I gasped, a tremor ripping through me at his soft touch. My knees went weak, and I bit back a whimper at how good it felt to simply *be* and allow another man to love on me for a change.

His tongue flickered over me a few times. "Taste even better."

"Jasper," I whispered, every inch of me shivering, his words of praise making my throat swell up tight.

One last chaste kiss to my puckered hole, and he stood. "Get your gorgeous ass on my bed, baby."

Heart pounding and insides quivering with anticipation, I did as told.

"On your back," he said while pulling off his shirt, revealing his trim build and smooth skin. "I want to watch your face while I work my dick inside your ass and make you mine."

I cursed and squeezed the base of my leaking cock, full of wonder over the seemingly delicate man whose filthy mouth caused my dick to leak like a damned faucet.

Jasper dropped his clothes to the floor while eyeing my body. "You're so beautiful."

"I'm old," I argued, unable to look away from his stiff, almost obscenely thick cock that jutted straight out from his prominent hip bones. My mouth watered and ass clenched at the thought of being stretched past the point of comfort.

He snorted. "Hardly. You're just prematurely gray, and I happen to love it. I find everything about you sexy as fuck." He climbed onto the mattress, and I spread my legs, making room for his lean frame.

I had at least six inches on him height-wise but not so many that our bodies didn't align where they needed to. His longer torso placed his hard dick against mine with only a slight reach for my mouth. He kissed me senseless, and I wrapped my legs around the backs of his thighs. We moved together, grinding and smearing pre-cum over each other.

If we continued to frot, I would paint our abs long before he offered me his dick.

"Need you," I murmured against his lips, so damn desperate to be filled by him.

"I've got you," Jasper said, shifting away, his lips trailing down my neck, to my clavicle where he nibbled and suckled until I begged him to mark me. He gave what I asked for, earning even more of my awe and appreciation.

He nuzzled his cheek against my chest hair. "So perfect," he murmured and placed a kiss atop my scar.

I stilled, but Jasper traced the *J* with his hot tongue as though laying claim over that part of my body as well.

A tear slid down my cheek. "Jasper—please."

He scooted to the side, reaching for his bedside table for supplies.

I trembled and fought to keep from losing my shit as he settled on his haunches between my thighs and rolled a condom over his length. "How much did you prep?"

"Only enough so I can enjoy the stinging stretch—"

Jasper sank two fingers deep inside me, cutting me off.

"Yes," I hissed, my eyes once more sliding shut in bliss.

"So tight." He nipped my upper thigh. "You're going to feel so good wrapped around my dick, Mase. I'm dying to bury my cock inside this hot hole."

Oh, God... He was going to be the death of me.

"Jasper." I grabbed his hair, forcing his focus off how my ass clutched at his fingers.

Amber eyes blazing with passion, he peered up over my body, our gazes latching. He stroked twice, fingertips grazing over my prostate with each pass. My dick bucked, a droplet of pre-cum dripping toward my tightened abs.

"I-I'm ready," I whispered.

Still holding my gaze, Jasper kissed my drawn-up balls.

I hissed.

He chuckled.

I glowered.

He outright laughed and nipped my thigh again. "So impatient."

"Damn right I am," I huffed. "I've been waiting for you for years."

And I wanted him for the rest of my life.

Chapter 14

Jasper

Mason had put on a front at Troy and Silas's, but with me and in the privacy of my home, he allowed his walls to lower so I could share in the emotions he experienced.

The connection between us transcended lust, and I didn't just ache to bury my dick in his body but to wrap our souls together, entwined with an unbreakable bond. We hadn't spoken of our feelings fully for one another, but our desire lay evident in every glance, every soft touch, and every hungry kiss.

Desperation had never felt so good, and he wasn't the only impatient one.

While I hadn't shared my secret desires for more feminine colors and clothing with Mason, I grew anxious to give him the parts of me that I could. Fear of him being turned off would keep me silent to the grave.

But I still had a lot to offer him.

Mason breathed harshly, fisting my sheets with a white-knuckled grip as though anchoring himself.

I wanted those hands on me. Clinging. Trusting me to hold him steady and fulfill his needs.

"You're perfect," I murmured, loving how he soaked in my words of praise. "Beautiful." Tucking three fingers deep inside his body, I licked up his abs, over his scar, nipped a tight nipple, and claimed his mouth.

He grabbed my hair, heels pressing along my legs as he attempted to move our hips where he wanted them.

"I'm going to take care of you," I murmured against his mouth while rubbing over his prostate.

Either he couldn't find words, or the leaking length of him between our stomachs readied to erupt, stealing his voice.

Sliding my fingers from his ass, I shifted, aligning the head of my cock with his relaxed hole. "Breathe, baby."

He inhaled on command, and I pushed in, finally— finally—becoming one with him.

"Jesus," he hissed, hazel eyes shaded with lust as my swollen head notched just inside his ring.

I licked over his parted lips, his panted exhales warming my face. "Okay?" I asked, my entire body tense and ready to shove in fully.

"So thick." He gulped. "Give me more, Jasper. Need to feel you inside me."

Lifting my head, I held his gaze and tunneled in with steady but slow force, claiming him exactly as I wanted to. Slick lube eased the way, allowing me to sink in without too much resistance until his heat clasped at my entire length.

"Jasper." His voice caught, and I settled atop him, taking his mouth.

My dick throbbed inside him, and my heart raced as he wrapped his legs around me, his arms clutching at my back.

We couldn't be closer. No space rested between us.

But it would never be enough.

"I won't ever get my fill of you," I murmured and licked at his tongue, trying to burrow deeper into his heart.

The need to move, to stroke, and to bring us both pleasure tingled through my spine. I began a slow rocking, allowing him to grow accustomed to my girth. While I didn't have length to brag about, I'd heard more than one complaint about how much I stretched a hole no matter how willing its owner.

But Mason took me with ease, moaning as though enjoying my thick cock.

"Fuck," I groaned, my eyelids finally fluttering closed. "You feel so good, Mason. Your hot little ass...mind-blowing. Want to burrow inside and never leave."

"Jasper." He breathed my name like a prayer, and I lifted to my elbows, needing to watch his face as I stroked inside him.

Passion-hazed eyes peered up at me, and I thrust a bit harder, making him gasp.

"Yes," he hissed, and I slammed home. "Fuck...Christ, Jasper—give it to me. Please."

I gifted what he asked for, deep-seated thrusts pulling grunts from his chest every time our groins slapped together. The scent of sex swarmed around us, his breaths panting over my mouth.

"Mase..." I couldn't put words to the emotion rolling through me, my desire to love him, to fulfill him. Taking his mouth, I poured my feelings into my kiss and in how I moved my hips.

He lifted to meet me, and I snaked a hand to his plump ass, angling to better tag his sweet spot.

"Ugh," he grunted, and I swallowed down the sound,

thrusting in the same way, the throbbing head of my dick rubbing over his prostate. "M-More," he stuttered the word against my mouth, the strength of his body wrapped around mine anchoring me in the moment when I wanted to soar.

"You were made for me, Mase," I murmured, catching his gaze while slamming into him. "So hot. Sexy. Feel how perfect our bodies are together?"

Mason bloomed at my words of praise, happiness radiating through the lust simmering between us.

I could fall for this man—if I hadn't already.

He completed me in every way, allowed me to become the protective caretaker I'd always longed to be. Mason didn't mind that I was smaller or younger. He got off on how my soft hands caressed him, how my thinner body loved on his.

Mason's cock leaked between our bodies, his slick and our sweat making for an easy, erotic glide. Every thrust of my hips jolted his length along our abs.

"Think you can come hands-free?" I managed through panted breaths, squeezing his lush ass in my palm while stabbing into his hole.

"Ohfuckyes," he slurred the words together as though drunk on my dick.

"Do it for me." I clasped his nape with my free hand, giving him my full weight and holding him in place. "I want your cum messy as fuck between us."

He hissed, and his eyelids closed, head tipping back.

I latched onto his neck, sucking hard—and he shuddered.

"Jas—" My name dissolved on his lips with a grunt, his body jerking beneath me, big dick bucking between our bodies. Heat erupted, coating our skin.

"Yes, baby—my lover," I crooned, continuing to hit his

prostate and prolong his release. "Fuck, you're so beautiful."

His hole pulsed around my cock, and I gritted my teeth to stave off what I knew would be the orgasm of a lifetime.

"Jasper," he gasped, clutching at my hair.

My hips stuttered. "Gonna—fuck I'm going to come."

"Yes." He lifted his head to claim my lips.

Tingles raced through my spine, straight to my taint. My balls seized, and Mason swallowed my curses, cradling me as I spasmed atop him. My body jerked in his firm hold, unable to escape him even if I wanted to. I didn't. Shudders ripped through me with the last spurt into the condom. Climaxing in him, surrounded by him, hadn't lasted nearly long enough.

Mason might be needy with me, but I was greedy as fuck for every inch of him.

"Shit." I gasped for breath, slumping atop him fully, my face in his neck. "My *God*."

He soothed his hands up and down my back, heels still locked behind my ass, keeping me in place.

No emotional barriers stood between us. Not a goddamn one. He'd let me in fully.

"You don't allow others a peek behind your mask," I murmured against his skin and kissed where I'd marked him. "But I know you, Mase. I *see* you."

"I lock myself up in public," he claimed, his voice raspy, "but with you...I feel truly safe for the first time in my life."

I squeezed him tight, lifting my head to press a soft kiss to his mouth. "You are, Mason. Always will be."

He had learned his lessons the hard way, same as I had.

I would make it my mission to pave a path ahead of us not just with good intentions but with an ease of passage he would be willing to walk down while holding my hand.

And nothing—not my own issues, his dysregulation, and

certainly not some spoiled stalker—would change our course headed toward the fulfillment we both longed for and deserved.

Chapter 15

Mason

Jasper took the next two days off work, and we spent the bulk of our hours in his bed, having those pillow talks I wanted and memorizing every inch of each other's bodies. He didn't mind my jealous need for his attention, how I clung to him to keep my demons at bay. His affection made me act like a starved kitten, all but purring and rubbing over him whenever I had the chance.

We fit in every way, so damn well I had difficulty trusting the reality I'd fallen into when I kept a piece of my past from him. Surely a wrecking ball of knowledge would come crashing through the bubble of our little world and ruin what we built together.

I feared its arrival. Strove to avoid it no matter the cost.

But I wasn't the only one with secrets.

While he showered our second evening together, I went searching for another bottle of lube since we'd emptied the partial he'd kept in his bedside table's top drawer. When I pulled open the bottom drawer, I blinked, taking a few seconds to recognize what I looked at.

Silk. Lace.

I pulled out a skimpy pair of pale pink panties, my mind immediately going haywire over the fact Jasper lied to me about being gay. Did he have a woman lover? An ex?

Swallowing hard, I grabbed another pair of underwear but noticed they weren't exactly cut for covering a female's parts. Plenty of room lay in the front area...as though the garment had been made specifically to cradle a cock.

"Huh." I stared, rubbing the material through my fingers, wondering...

Jasper, while a strict top, tended to give off a more bottom vibe with his higher voice and how he moved with feminine grace. Perhaps I judged, but I couldn't help the stereotypes carved into my head since childhood. Had he not told me his preference, I would have sworn he enjoyed having his ass filled.

Did Jasper have a panties kink? I could see it. My cock appreciated the thought. Why hadn't he shared that part of him with me if it was true?

He knew everything—well, *almost* everything—about me that mattered. Jasper and I had agreed that conquests and hookups prior to one another belonged in the past and would hold no bearing on our future.

But this...

The shower turned off, and I stuffed the panties back into the drawer, quietly shutting it while telling my cock to calm the fuck down. I didn't want to upset Jasper by prying, especially after our peaceful escape together.

Time would bring us closer, allow him to open up to me in ways it appeared he hid from me. But I was certainly curious how far his desire for pretty things went.

Did it bother him that I called him that word? Pretty rather than handsome? Since he was a smaller, gentle man, I expected I wasn't the first—I definitely wouldn't be the last.

I crawled between the fresh sheets we'd put on his bed prior to climbing into the shower, and closed my eyes, willing away the image of Jasper in pink lace panties from my mind.

"Someone is sleepy," he murmured a few moments later while snuggling up against my backside.

"You wore my ass out."

"Mmm," his rumbled noise of approval made me smile, but his stroke over my backside, his fingers sliding through my crack encouraged a moan to rise from my chest. "Love your ass." Jasper nipped my shoulder, and I pressed back into him.

Love everything about you, I wanted to whisper but didn't.

"Get some rest, baby," he murmured and kissed me again. "Your delicious hole needs a break. I'll stretch you out in the morning. Hell, maybe I'll wake you up by sinking deep into your ass."

"Jasper," I groaned.

He chuckled. "Sleep."

Eyes closed, I relaxed in his protective arms, hoping he would keep my mind from rousing memories.

I knew I dreamed by the hazy way my eyes perceived what went on around me—where I lay. Spread-eagle on a mattress, ankles and wrists bound to bedposts, I shivered with bone-clattering tremors. I had agreed to be tied for his pleasure.

Satisfy the customer.

The red flags hadn't mattered. The sixth sense, my need for self-preservation had been shoved aside in my loyalty to Micah and Elite.

Joseph sat on my aching groin, but he looked more like a demon than angel, his red eyes burning into me from my periphery with searing fire. I couldn't keep my focus on him, but he held me captive while taking what I didn't wish to give.

He owned my body, controlled my fear. Manipulated me with lies, making me question my desires, even the denials pouring from my lips.

"N-No," I whispered, trying to sink into the mattress, away from the gleaming blade dripping molten metal onto my chest.

My skin sizzled—burned with agony that caused me cry out.

"P-Please don't," I pleaded as he leaned over me, wetness smearing between our bodies.

You're mine. Always and forever.

I shook my head, desperate to escape his evil, hissing voice, his agonizing touch that sliced through my skin as he marked me.

This cock. This body. This mind. He spoke over my mouth, the scent of burning flesh and brimstone flooding my lungs, stealing my breath. *Every inch of you belongs to me.*

"Help me!" I cried out, twisting and thrashing to escape him, but his weight atop me, the bindings around me, held tight.

Freedom was nothing but a dream, Joseph's ownership of my entire being reality.

"Mason."

"No!" I hollered, tears heating my face as I clenched my eyes shut against the vision of him writhing atop me.

A tender caress on my cheek—

Couldn't trust it.

I jerked my head away, desperate for space to breathe. To exist as *me*, not a prisoner of another's evil desires.

"Mason, baby." A voice choked out the words with pain similar to the ache spreading through my chest. "I'm here."

I gasped, my eyelids flying upward.

The image of Joseph in my mind's eye, his manic expression, moved like a heat wave... shimmering...dissolving.

Gentle touches to my neck, my shoulder drew me from the darkness of my memories. A hand ran over my hair, fingers working through the strands. Fingernails grazed my scalp, sending a shiver down my spine and helping me focus on the present.

"Shh. I'm here," the sweet voice repeated. "I have you."

Jasper.

I swallowed hard and burst into a sob as I focused on his amber eyes. "Hold me," I gasped, reaching to draw him close. We clung together, and I couldn't burrow deep enough into his embrace. Couldn't sear his touch into my soul as thoroughly as Joseph had. Couldn't weave the fabric of our beings into one where nothing had access to me but him.

My tears eventually dried, and still Jasper held me. His lips pressed to my hair as I exhaled a shuddered sigh against his warm neck. He smelled like sunshine and freedom even after hours of sleep.

Jasper was my savior sent from heaven to rescue me from the hellish spawn who tormented my mind. If only I could find release from my past trauma and emotional healing through his touch.

"Okay now?" he murmured, his breath hot on my forehead.

I nodded, awake and aware I'd escaped my nightmare but was far from stable.

"Do you want to talk about it?"

My throat swelled from rising panic. The truth of that night, how I had become bound and at Joseph's mercy, was the last thing Jasper needed to hear from my lips.

I would lose him for sure.

Shaking my head, I pressed closer against him, nuzzling his neck. "Make me forget."

Jasper didn't speak a word, simply gave me what I asked for, saving me from haunting memories and creating new ones to take their place.

If only they could be enough to last me through the weeks to come.

Kellen got back from Maine on the day my lover reluctantly returned to his office.

I went home and tidied up according to the chart Jasper had left me. After taking the lazy way out and ordering groceries rather than heading out into public for them myself where I might buckle beneath anxiety, I settled on the couch.

I still hadn't told my friend about the assault, deciding to wait until his brief vacation ended, since I knew he would be upset.

The guilt of withholding the full truth from Jasper ate at my insides. If I didn't find relief soon, I would end up with an ulcer.

At least the texts from Joseph had stopped after the initial influx on Sunday, so I didn't need a harassment order.

It appeared as though I had dropped off the face of the earth for my tormentor. Perhaps he'd given up on me and had found a new daddy, someone as kinky and fucked up in the head as he was. If so, he would leave me alone, allowing me freedom to hope for a future with Jasper.

Rather than telling Kellen over the phone what had happened after I'd left Micah's party, I shot him a text.

Me: **What are you up to?**

Kell: **Nothing. I don't have a client until later tonight, so I'm free.**

Me: **Lunch?**

Kell: **Want to whip up some of your famous waffles or should I grab a couple of steak bombs?**

My mouth watered at his suggestion. It had been weeks since I'd had a sub from Antonio's, and Jasper had made my favorite breakfast every morning after waking me up with his lips around my dick.

Me: **Steak bombs. TY**

He sent back a thumbs up as was typical, and I wasted the following minutes folding the laundry that had been sitting in a basket for a week. Washing clothes had been fifty times easier at Jasper's. He had the appliances in an actual laundry room instead of a musty basement that no one respected.

Being separated from Jasper made me antsy, but the initial anxiety that attempted to swallow me whole after the attack had lessened to the point I could at least function without having to hold his hand. But going out into public by myself? I wasn't yet ready for that step.

Kellen showed up with the subs and gave me a bro hug, which I enjoyed while it lasted. He was one of my—if not only—friends, and as usual, he dressed in all black and always looked so damn put together.

While a lot of the EEMM guys hung out when not on the clock, I'd never felt as though I fit in enough to bullshit with my façade for any length of time. Especially if booze got involved. I wasn't sure I would be able to keep my confident, daddy silver fox mask in place.

We weren't sitting at my cleared table for two minutes before he asked if I'd talked to Micah about the hotel shooting. Answering that question led to the truth that I hadn't actually escaped unscathed and had been assaulted.

"Why didn't you call me from the hospital?" he asked, his lips thinning immediately after.

"You were leaving for Maine."

"I would have cancelled to help you out, Mason."

My face heated, and I didn't bother trying to hide my feelings. "Jasper stayed with me."

"The guy who stopped the attack?"

"Yeah."

Kellen's gaze narrowed, but his lips quirked. "You're smiling."

I cleared my throat and shrugged. "We've been together every day since."

"As in he's been watching over you? Taking care of you?"

"Well, that too, but—*together*, together."

One of his eyebrows popped up. "What about Elite?"

I fiddled with my sub's paper wrapper. "I...uh talked to Micah. He told me to take some time off. I didn't plan on making a decision about staying on as an escort until I figured out if Jasper and I might have a future or not."

"And?"

I glanced up to find Kellen studying my face. He'd been my friend for years, and I'd never once truly opened up to him, shared about my childhood, or how it had impacted my adult life. He'd only ever seen the fake Mason, the persona I put on for strangers.

"I owe you an apology."

His brows furrowed as he sat back in his chair. "What for?"

"Being a lousy friend. There's a lot I haven't told you about myself, Kellen."

"You don't need to uncover any secrets you have, Mason. Some shit is private. I've seen you anxious and unsettled even though you try to hide your emotions, but I don't need to know the why."

"You have?"

"I've been involved in your life long enough that I can read past that front you put on around other people."

I let out a steady exhale, relaxing in my seat. "I need to tell you everything so you can give me some advice."

Kellen nodded, and I proceeded to explain about Joseph Delaney, the truth of who had attacked me Friday night, and the fact I hadn't yet shared with Jasper what I'd done for work since January.

He rubbed along his scruff, nodding as though he understood what I faced. "That's a tough situation you're in, my friend."

"Jasper says there's nothing that will veer us off the path we're on, but being an Elite isn't a small matter. And yeah, I have every intention of giving up my job for a future with him, but..."

"You're afraid he's going to leave you if he finds out."

"Very." I swallowed hard, shoving against panic that wanted to rise and shut me down. My fingers itched for Jasper's to cling to. "He's...everything to me. A perfect fit for all my needs."

He barked a laugh. "A cute, needy twink who can't get enough of your big dick?"

Kellen had most of that right.

"While he *is* smaller and younger than me—" I attempted a smile "—I'm actually the bottom."

Kellen blinked, his grin wiped from his face. "What?"

Trying to shrug it off didn't work. "Being on the receiving end has always been my preference. I actually dislike topping."

"The fuck, Mason?" Kellen stared. "You're Elite's most-wanted daddy. All you *do* is top!"

"Thank fuck for the endless supply of little blue pills," I stated bluntly, nervous that Kellen would see me in a different light too.

"Shit." Kellen chuckled though, easing my tensed insides. "I thought I had you figured out. Does anyone else know?"

"No. It's nobody's business but mine. With Elite, Micah took one look at me and cast me into a role he said would bring in the big bucks—and I needed all I could get to help support my sister's family."

She was one part of my life Kellen *had* been aware of, which was why he'd recommended Elite in the first place. Lots of cash for minimal hours worked.

"So Jasper is the daddy in your relationship," Kellen mused, shaking his head as though still unable to process the bomb I'd dropped.

I rolled my eyes. "You know I'm not into any kinky shit. He's not my daddy, but he does take care of me. It fulfills a part of him no one has given him the opportunity to do before."

Kellen studied my face, a soft smile on his lips. "And he does the same for you. Your eyes don't ever lie."

"I'm over the fucking moon for him. That's why this truth I'm keeping from him is killing me."

"Then you have to tell him, Mason," Kellen said, his tone low and serious as he leaned onto the table with his elbows, arms crossed. "The sooner the better. Continuing to hide this is only going to fill you with more anxiety. And if

Jasper can't get over that you escorted men around as your means of earning a living, then it would be better if he left now instead of a year down the road when your lives are fully intertwined and your heart would pay the price."

"That will already happen at this point," I muttered past the thickness in my throat.

"Then I'll be here for you to help put the pieces back together in whatever way I can."

While I appreciated the sentiment, I hoped it wouldn't come to that.

Chapter 16

Jasper

Troy showed up at my office to take me out to lunch. While we hadn't made plans in advance, I'd been overrun with work from having missed so much and needed a break.

"How are things with you and Mason?" he asked as we settled at a table in a small bistro a few blocks from Humanity House.

Memories of the previous few days swamped my mind, warming me through. I smiled even though I envied Troy's pink button-down and striped tie I would never have the balls to wear. "Incredible. It's crazy how well we get along, how smooth everything has gone considering the circumstances behind our meeting."

"The honeymoon stage is always like that."

I huffed a snort. "Please. You've been with Silas for two years now, and you're still as in love with each other as when you first figured out that what you felt for one another wasn't just lust."

Our waitress interrupted to take our orders, and Troy

went right to what we'd been discussing once she moved away.

"Our love hasn't changed, but as we've gotten to know one another better, we've realized sharing a life together isn't just rainbows and unicorns. We've had dozens of fights. It's getting beyond the things that rub us the wrong way and learning how to deal with them that makes for a strong relationship."

"I'm sure issues will pop up with Mason that annoy me, but we're so good together," I insisted, my heart light, my voice earnest. "He's the only man who has ever let me top in every way, Troy. He *likes* giving me control. It's something he needs that he's never had before and vice versa. He looks at me like I'm the best thing since sliced bread. What we have is almost...*too* perfect."

"What do you know about him? His past?" Troy didn't sound convinced, his pale blue eyes studying my face intently.

"Everything about his childhood is familiar to me. We've experienced the same setbacks and heartaches. The level of empathy between us is amazing," I insisted. "And he's completely open and honest with his emotions too. There's no guessing with that man. No games for a change."

Our waitress set our drink orders on the table and left us in peace once more.

I couldn't keep the grin off my face. Even though returning to work had been overwhelming, I felt an inner peace and happiness that transcended stress, all thanks to the new man in my life.

Troy took a sip of his water with lemon, eyeing me without a hint of happiness in his eyes.

"What?" I asked, my smile faltering slightly, the hum of the busy restaurant around us fading away.

Lips in a thin line, he set his glass aside and pulled out his cell phone. Swiping it to life, he asked, "Have you checked out Mason online? Done any digging to make sure he's being honest with you?"

"What?" Another puff of laughter left my lungs, but my smile diminished as Troy once more turned his serious gaze to my face.

"Has he told you what he's really been doing for work since Carter Communications folded in January?"

"Odd jobs," I replied. "Nothing permanent—but he did check out Silas's website and is considering putting in an application for the new team members they're looking for. He seems to think he might be a good fit."

Troy slid his cell across the table, and the hairs on my nape rose with some sixth sense of impending...something I wouldn't like.

"What's this?" I picked his phone up with a shaking hand.

A picture of a shirtless Mason...

I glanced to the website's title. *Elite Escorts MM.* I scrolled down, reading and not comprehending the description of the man who had stolen my heart.

"He's an escort, Jasper," Troy stated quietly, leaning forward to speak for my ears alone. "He's Elite's most sought-after silver fox, a dick for hire who cares for men who have a lot of money to blow on make-believe sugar daddies."

I stared at the picture of my lover, the body I recognized. Had memorized. "That's—that's *not* Mason," I argued over the description my friend had recited to me.

"It is."

"But...he's not even a top! What the fuck is this, Troy?" Scowling, I clicked the website's menu and perused the front page, convinced it was some kind of hoax. A very *unfunny* April Fool's joke in July.

It wasn't.

EEMM was an actual escort service—posh as hell and definitely only available for those well above my pay grade. Over a dozen available escorts were listed according to whatever a client desired. Arm candy. Simple dinner date. Vanilla to the opposite end of the sexual spectrum of sadist dom.

Mason's profile listed him as Elite's sexy silver fox with raving reviews about his professionalism and agreeable nature. The persona he wore in public sat like a mask on his face...

I tore my focus off his fake smile in the picture, my chest aching—fucking cracking in two. He'd lied? I'd thought... fuck, I'd trusted the connection we had between us.

Did I really though, my inner voice whispered. I hadn't shared my secrets with him either and had no plans to. It would be best to keep the truth from him to protect the little boy inside me my father had bullied and nearly beaten half to death.

"I-I don't understand. He hasn't said anything about this," I choked out, my eyes stinging.

Wariness filled Troy's gaze. "I'm guessing he feels ashamed about his work, but it also makes me wonder what else he hasn't told you."

Fuck. "Y-you think there's more?"

Troy shrugged.

I swallowed hard, fighting for calm. "How did you find this?"

"I'm a lawyer. I'm curious about everything. Suspicious. And when it comes to my friends..." Troy shrugged again without an ounce of apology in his gaze. "You're a good man, Jasper. I don't want to see you get hurt."

I hadn't ever asked Mason what he had been doing at the hotel on the night he'd been attacked. I glanced back down at his false front I recognized all too well. Had he been with a client? Or was the fake part of Mason Thomson the one *I* knew and was falling for and that image I stared at was the truth?

My stomach churned as I grasped for an explanation, his unwillingness to share the truth with me. I'd thought Mason trusted me fully, that he'd let me in. Had I been manipulated by a master as his mom had been? But for what, exactly? It sure as fuck wasn't cash. I didn't have enough money to even afford an hour of his time.

I couldn't believe that. No. I *had* seen the real Mason. I'd held him while he sobbed in my arms the night before, a man broken down. I'd watched the lingering nightmare fade from his eyes while sinking into his body, claiming his full focus. I'd made love to a man who worked as an escort for the rich...

Puzzle pieces slid together in my mind as I focused on him rather than my own hurt.

"Fuck." I rubbed a hand over my face and pushed the cell back across the table to Troy. "His stalker was a client, wasn't he?"

"When Mason mentioned the Delaney boy, I decided to have Silas's guy Chavéz do a little digging. The kid is trouble, and while a daddy is exactly what he needs in real life, his lifestyle showcased on social media doesn't match up with the man Mason seems to be: decent, well-spoken, and the settle-down type."

What was the real story about that evening...and the

initial carved into Mason's chest? The man I'd had in my bed for the last three nights was not a top and yet he sold his dick to satisfy customers needing a little TLC under a daddy bear?

Swallowing, I tried to process the truth and how to go about moving forward.

"What—what am I supposed to do with this?" I asked, not really looking for an answer. My brain still struggled to accept what I'd learned.

Troy leaned fully onto the table, his steady gaze reaching deep into my soul. "Do you love him?"

"I-I'm not sure," I muttered, slumping in my chair as doubt once more crowded my mind. "I could. Easily. But what if everything I know about him isn't true?"

"What if it is?"

"Huh?"

"What if what Mason has told you *is* true, and he's simply left out some facts because he's ashamed of escorting and playing an unsatisfying part just for money?"

Mason definitely dealt with all sorts of unwanted, uncomfortable emotions. I couldn't begin to imagine his concern and anxiety over the truth becoming known to the man he saw as his savior.

Did he honestly believe I would judge him? We'd discussed at length about how our pasts shaped us. How choices lead us in directions we were meant to traverse in learning how to move forward onto our next path in life.

Why would a man such as him resort to selling his dick though, especially when he called himself a strict bottom? While I didn't look down on a person or their choices in life, what had made Mason that desperate?

He'd lost his job in January. He'd never been in a

serious relationship because, like me, he'd been unable to find someone who fit in with his desires. Had he been so hungry for attention and physical touch that he signed on with Elite just to have some of his needs met?

But that wouldn't make sense because of how he'd been cast according to Elite's website—the last thing he would find with clients would be true physical fulfillment like he found by being stuffed by my dick.

"I'm so damn lost right now," I whispered. "I have so many questions. I just...don't understand."

"Does the fact he hid this from you change how you feel about him?"

I shook my head. "I won't ever judge a man for his past."

"Then talk to him. Explain that to him. Maybe it really is something as simple as shame that kept him from telling you, but like a friend told me once, grab life ball the balls. Holler a 'Gimme!' and take what you want." A soft smile curved Troy's lips. "Don't let him react in his emotions and make him see your acceptance. He seems the sort that would need to feel valued."

Troy had no idea the truth he spoke, but he'd nailed Mason's personality down with his statement. And that last bit? It totally applied to me as well.

"Thank you for looking out for me," I said, forcing myself to inhale a deep breath and attempt to calm my racing heart.

"Anything for you, my friend."

Our waitress returned with our food, and my stomach turned over at the thought of eating.

"Want to take this to go?" Troy asked, his voice quiet and understanding.

I nodded, eyeing the chicken ziti broccoli I had ordered.

"Yeah. I...I think I need to sit in silence for a while and make sense of all this in my brain. Then I'm heading over to Mason's to find out what's really going on."

Hopefully, he would be honest, and we could work through whatever this obstacle proved to be.

Chapter 17

Mason

My palms sweated.

I eyed the digital clock on my microwave from where I sat ramrod stiff at my kitchen table. Not long after Kellen had left, Jasper texted me that he was bringing dinner over a little early.

I planned on taking Kellen's advice and telling him the truth. About Elite. Joseph.

Swallowing against rising bile, I counted my breaths, trying to calm myself. I wanted to escape. Shut down and ignore the one hurdle keeping me fully from Jasper.

Would he hate me?

Be disgusted by me?

Never trust me again?

I'd outright lied about what I'd been doing since January, so he had every right to walk away without looking back. My childhood had taught me that some truths were better left unsaid so your emotions couldn't be manipulated, but I'd fucked up big time. What I wanted with Jasper—complete inhibition and comfort with him—would only come from laying all my cards on the table.

Would he accept what most people would consider a shameful part of my past? Would he be able to see beyond the way I'd chosen to sell my body in order to help my sister and her family survive? My decision hadn't been solely for her—I couldn't blame her for my actions. I'd hoped in the beginning to find some sense of satisfaction in sex.

I hadn't.

And now I might lose the best thing I'd ever found because of it.

Jasper's quiet knock caused me to jolt to my feet, and rubbing my palms down my shorts, I approached the door. My heart pounded. Mouth dried.

Please...please somehow make this okay.

I pulled the door open, and Jasper's lack of smile, his wary eyes flitting over my face had my heart bottoming out. Anxiety rose to choke off my air.

"Mason," he greeted quietly, no peace in his gaze or his tone when he looked at me.

I stepped back, tongue-tied and floundering on the edge of a shutdown.

He moved past me, set a takeout bag on the table, and turned toward me.

Unmoving, door still open, knob clenched in my hand, I stared. He was so beautiful. Smooth face, big, soulful amber eyes, the petite nose that crinkled when he smiled, and the softest lips I dreamed about kissing forever.

"I-I have to tell you something," I choked out, on the verge of plummeting. Or puking. Probably both.

A huge exhale sagged Jasper's shoulders, the slight furrow between his eyebrows relaxing. "Why don't you shut the door and sit with me."

I nodded but didn't move.

With a smile that didn't quite light up his eyes, Jasper

approached me, eased my hold from the door, and pressed it shut behind me. "Come on, baby."

The nickname brought tears of relief to my eyes, and the steadying grip of his hand on mine eased the clench in my stomach. I followed like a meek lamb as Jasper led me into the living room. He sat first, tugging me down beside him.

I angled so my knee pressed to his, needing another point of contact between us besides our hands.

"Talk to me, Mase. Tell me what's causing your unrest, and we'll see if we can't make you feel better."

"I want that more than anything," I whispered, unable to look at his face. Instead, I studied my white knuckles from how tightly I gripped his fingers.

"Nothing you can say to me will change this connection between us, Mason. I've told you that before."

My nod felt more like a flinch.

"So just spill it. Let's work through this together."

Closing my eyes, I inhaled fully so I wouldn't pass out from lack of oxygen. What I had to share needed to tumble out on one breath, or I would never get through it.

"Before I met you, I worked as an escort, and Joseph was a client. He paid for me—I topped him, and he wasn't the only one."

My pulse thrummed, and I swallowed hard, waiting for Jasper to detangle our hands, for him to sneer and tell me what a sick bastard I was, to scream at me for lying to him.

He sat silent, unmoving.

Had he not heard me?

I peeked open an eyelid to find him studying my face with a gentle expression.

"Is that everything?"

As if that hadn't been bad enough...

I shook my head. "Those are the big parts. The impor-tant ones that will make you hate me."

"I would never, Mason."

"But...but men paid for me to be someone I wasn't—and I agreed. I fucked strangers for cash, Jasper, more than once. Hell, upwards of at least fifty times over the past six months."

He took in that information as though that fact didn't kick his guts like the low blow I'd expected it to be.

"You said that was before the night of the attack, right?" Jasper asked.

I nodded.

"Were you with a client that evening?"

"No—I was at a friend's birthday party."

"Did you have plans of going back to work for Elite after we met?"

I opened my mouth but snapped it shut before answer-ing. I hadn't once mentioned Elite to him.

Jasper's gaze remained open and vulnerable while my stomach clenched up tight.

"H-How long have you known?" I whispered.

"Just today."

"Why...why aren't you flipping out? Why aren't you at least glaring at me or running to the bathroom to puke because the idea of what I've done makes you sick?"

Jasper caressed his palm over my whiskers, and I leaned into his touch without thought, eyes once more welling with tears. "You signed on with Elite because it was a lucrative job, didn't you?"

I nodded, unable to speak.

"Did you also initially think that you might find some sort of sexual gratification in that line of work?"

I figured that I could claim to be vers to get the job, then maybe actually get to bottom on occasion. After my first meeting with Micah and seeing his excitement over adding a daddy to his menu, I'd signed for the money alone, my hope put in its place. "I knew what the job would entail after my interview."

"And yet you still agreed to work for Elite."

"Yes," I whispered, "because of Marin and her family."

"I don't care how you chose to support your sister," Jasper stated firmly, scooting closer to grasp my chin. "The fact you love her enough to do whatever necessary to help keep food on their table says a lot about your character, Mason."

Tears dripped off my chin even though I couldn't hold onto or name any of the many emotions swirling inside me.

"Have you been tested recently?"

Jasper and I had used condoms every time we'd had sex, but I understood his concern.

"Last Thursday after meeting with a client, and I was given the all clear," I assured him, swiping an arm over my wet eyes. "Elite requires biweekly bloodwork and condoms for employees and PrEP for the MM branch. We aren't allowed to go without."

"And you haven't been with anyone but me since your last results?"

"No."

"Will you tell me the rest? Everything else you're ashamed of or feel you ought to be embarrassed about?"

I studied Jasper's intense gaze, the lack of judgment, his desire to understand me fully. A sense of peace stole over the unease wrecking my insides, bringing quiet calm. Hope that we might be okay after all. I blew out a heavy exhale. "You want to know about Joseph."

"If it would help to talk about the experience and get better closure, then yes."

Kellen had told me to be honest, to share everything with Jasper—and I wanted to be relieved of the entire burden I'd carried for what seemed like years rather than almost three weeks.

Joseph had drugged my drink, and whatever it was had made my dick harder than any blue pill. It had also caused the rest of my body to become compliant, my mind on the edge of euphoria. I hadn't appreciated being drugged like that, but the boy loved to party, and I'd been paid to please him. Thinking of the money that would be dropped in my bank account, I'd agreed to being tied up.

"Perhaps a part of me had hoped Joseph would want to take being in charge to another level...that maybe he would top me, but he went beyond fucked up. He changed into a fairy princess outfit—a sparkly, pink tutu, satin jockstrap, and iridescent wings strapped to his back."

Jasper shifted at my description of Joseph's attire, his tension palpable, but he didn't interrupt.

"Rather than giving me what I'd wanted, he rode me twice instead, denying me an orgasm both times."

"Jesus Christ," Jasper choked on the words before swallowing hard.

I plowed forward, needing to just get the story out. No longer hidden so I could finally be free.

"Once bored, he moved on to his other kink beyond ropes. His knife. While sitting on my chest, he'd bragged about its cost and how he'd gotten off on drawing blood from men like me. I—I'd begged him to untie me, but he ignored my pleadings and took his knife to my chest. I'd never seen such manic light in a person's eyes before, nor had I heard such sick words of claiming."

"Mason—"

"No." I shook my head. "I—I have to finish. Please."

Jasper's amber eyes were tortured, and the hitch in his shoulders made me want to crush him to my chest and offer *him* comfort.

"Nothing you've done or said has reminded me of him—nothing," I reiterated. "You make me forget. Give me new, better memories."

Lips pressed tightly, Jasper glanced away and nodded. "Tell me the rest, Mason," he whispered, his eyes shutting. "Every fucking thing he did. I-I have to hear it."

"His untouched cock pulsed cum while he'd carved his initial into me. I puked while screaming for him to stop, then again when he sliced across his own chest, just enough to cause red droplets to well at his wound. He laid atop me, smearing our blood and his seed together, claiming something about a deep bond that no one would ever be able to break. How I would be his forever. I passed out at that point." I still clutched Jasper's hand, needing his touch to keep me from falling back into the vivid memories in my mind. "When I woke up, I'd been untied, cleaned, and bandaged. The drugs had worn off, and I felt nothing but exhaustion with a fuzzy recollection of what had gone down. Like my mom, Joseph had manipulated me when I'd questioned what he'd done. He attempted to twist my memory of the incident to make me think I had somehow been in the wrong, not him.

"It wasn't until a few days later that I realized my shame, the pain, was due to falling for his emotional abuse. That I'd allowed someone, a much younger man, to control my feelings when I'd had years of practice at remaining unmoved by a narcissist. In that moment, I recognized the full extent of my weakness, and I have been struggling ever since to gain the sense of self he stole from me."

Jasper's throat worked for a few seconds before he found his voice. "You are one of the strongest men I know," he rasped, his eyes on our clasped hands.

Tears once more slid down my cheeks, and I burrowed into his chest, choosing to believe his lie.

Chapter 18

Jasper

When I'd first knocked on the door—hell, even driving to Mason's apartment, I'd been burdened by riotous thoughts. Not sure what to believe. Had Mason played me for a chump because I'd been so quick to trust him? Was he simply a product of his mom's manipulations and took back control by doing the same to others?

I just couldn't see it being that way, and the second he had opened the door to my knock, the tumultuous emotions rolling off him had told me all I needed to know. Like Troy had suggested, Mason had been truthful with me—but not completely.

One look in his tortured eyes, and I'd forgiven him. Trusted him as I'd done since the evening we'd met.

And the shit Mason had spewed at my insistence...

Fear and anger both rolled through me, but I focused on the latter.

I wanted to slice Joseph's balls off and shove them up his greedy ass. Then I would cut out the little cunt's lying tongue and fuck his throat with it until he choked to death.

Good riddance.

I'd never considered hurting someone in retaliation, but that punk ass kid who had abused Mason and had broken down the confidence he'd gained since escaping the prison of his childhood home? I wanted to inflict ten times the physical and emotional pain Joseph had Mason.

He'd done so while dressed as a fairy. Wearing *pink*. A damned satin jockstrap of which I owned more than one.

That image he'd painted in my head, along with the secrets I hid from my lover, caused bile to rise. I forced my focus elsewhere, swallowing against my need to vomit. Hearing what had happened to him solidified in my mind that part of me needed to be left in the past, never to be resurrected.

If he knew I dreamed of being free to let my feminine side shine, he would be reminded of Joseph—and be disgusted beyond what even my father had been. And the last thing I wanted to do was wear something that might trigger Mason and possibly send him spiraling again.

Disappointment wanted to creep in, but my beautiful man needed me fully in the moment, emotionally available. I would sacrifice that small part of what made me happy if it meant helping my lover find healing from his wounds.

"Is Elite's owner aware of what happened that night you spent with his client?" I asked, running my fingers up and down his spine, thankfully soothing my own mind by caressing him in the way he loved.

He stayed plastered to my chest, his body at an awkward, twisted angle. For the first time since meeting him, I wished he was smaller than me so he could cuddle on my lap.

"Yes. That's what I needed to call Micah about after we left the police station on Sunday. He's Elite's owner. It was why I didn't invite you up here—I didn't want you to know the truth. I'm sorry for lying about the odd jobs."

I kissed his hair again. "I forgive you, Mason."

"Just like that?"

"Just like that," I assured him while peeling him away from me. I settled back onto the couch, keeping hold of his hand for a continued connection between us.

"You're too good to me," he murmured, not looking at me.

"No," I correct him gently, "I'm exactly what you need —same as you are for me."

Tears once more welled in his eyes. "You probably think I'm a baby with how much I cry. I'm forty-two for fuck's sake."

"It's okay to have and express emotions," I murmured while smoothing his hair from his forehead. "And it's healthy to allow those you've bottled up for so long find release."

He leaned into my touch like he always did. "It's scary how much I want you—only you can save me."

"I can't be the one to put your pieces back together, Mason—I can't be your savior. You're going to have to do that on your own."

"How? Tell me what to do, and I'll do it," Mason begged, tears still rolling down his cheeks.

"You can focus on the little things like that chart I made for you, but you will benefit the most by seeing a therapist," I said. "And I know the perfect one, someone I can promise will listen, will be understanding, and will never judge you for your past."

I told Mason about Zeke, and while my friend didn't practice outside Humanity House, I knew he would take on seeing Mason for me if I asked. I didn't trust anyone else with Mason's fragile emotions.

Zeke would have the tools to help Mason. He would be able to guide him in growing in self-awareness, forgiving himself, and eventually finding healing.

"I-I think I would like that," Mason agreed. "But only because he's your friend."

"What did Micah say to you about pressing charges?" I asked, taking us back to the last bit of the story I wanted closure with.

"He said to do whatever I needed to."

"He will support you either way? Didn't try to talk you out of it or anything?" I needed clarity.

"Yes he does, and no, he didn't tell me to keep quiet about the affair." Mason studied our clasped hands, his free hand's index finger sliding along the grooves and dips between our skin in a self-calming gesture. "Elite isn't an illegal business, and Micah said that fact would hold no matter the scrutiny an investigation might bring. But when it comes right down to it, I just don't think I can face having to deal with Joseph and an ongoing case for months on end because that's how long it will take. His father will make it a bigger deal than it would have been even because of the Delaney name. I...I just don't have the strength for that."

"So you're leaning toward a no?"

Mason nodded—then shrugged. "I hate that Joseph will get away with this, but..."

"I understand." And I totally did. Mason would be a basket case even though I would be by his side every hour we spent in the courtroom. "Come on." I slid off the couch and tugged him up to his feet.

"Where are we going?"

"To eat the dinner I brought."

"I'm not really that hungry." Mason sounded exhausted. Hung out to dry and ready to call it quits for the night—exactly as I was.

I pulled out his chair and physically guided him to sit. "You need some food, baby."

I divided the chicken ziti broccoli I hadn't eaten after my lunch date with Troy. We each had a half piece of garlic bread too. A quick pop in the scrubbed-out microwave heated both plates to a more manageable temperature to force down.

Neither of us were in the mood to eat, but I'd spoken the truth. After the emotions of the day, we needed sustenance to keep clearer minds...and maybe energy should our night evolve into more than spilling and attempting to clean internal shit to the best of our abilities.

"Why are you okay with my history with Elite?" Mason asked quietly, his voice unsure.

I glanced up from my meal to find him studying me. "There have been dozens of people over the years—especially teenagers—who have come through Humanity House's doors who've done the same as you. They didn't have the controlled environment, the contracts, the reimbursement an Elite employee does, but I've witnessed the shame of sex workers before. I've seen the desperation that causes people to make the choices they do. You did what you had to at that moment in your life, Mason, and even if you'd done it for the money alone, I wouldn't judge you." I held his gaze, searching his face, hesitant but needing to broach one last topic.

Mason quitting Elite.

I'd wanted to save the conversation for a later date when I was more comfortable expressing verbally how I felt about him. We had shared dreams of a future but had yet to put a label on us as a couple or map out an agreed plan moving forward.

"I understand why you became an escort," I stated with firm intent, "but I won't condone your continuation in that line of work if we're going to be together."

His gaze flitted over my face, hope shining in eyes welling with tears. "You want me regardless of the mess I am? The drama I can't seem to escape?"

"I *always* want you," I murmured with a smile even though a part of me cried inside. I'd hoped to be comfortable enough, confident in Mason's feelings for me, to eventually share my secrets with him. But what Joseph Delaney had done ruined that dream for good. "Every minute of the day."

"Goddamnit, Jasper." He chuckled, swiping his forearm over his face. "The things you say to me don't even seem real." He laughed again. "Yes—Yes, I'll quit Elite because I want to be with you too. *Only* you. I haven't even thought of another man since the moment our gazes met."

"So." I reached across the table and threaded my fingers through his. "Boyfriends?"

"Yes, Jasper." Mason's eyes appeared more green than hazel from lingering moisture.

I lifted our hands and kissed his fingertips. "I think I'm falling in love with you."

"I've already fallen," Mason claimed, the energy between us intensifying, heating and coiling around my groin. "Can I show you how much?"

My dick swelled, and I nodded.

Cleaning up our dinner dishes could wait.

I didn't want Mason on his knees in case his desire to show me his love came from a subconscious need to express to me how sorry he was. Yearning to solidify what I'd claimed deep in his soul drove me to action.

Rather than sitting on the couch and letting him blow me in an act of servitude I knew he'd been wanting, I led him back to his bedroom. We didn't speak as we undressed, but with how our thoughts seemed intertwined, we moved together, peeling each other's clothes off. Sharing kisses. Soft touches.

When he reached for my hard length, I stopped him. One day, I would allow him to pleasure me, to be the giver, but not now. Not when emotions still ran high, and I might be tempted to question his intentions.

"On the bed, baby."

He obeyed without hesitation, so damn eager to please.

I guided him to lay down, taking the time to appreciate his body from forehead to toes. Every inch of him filled my senses—the warmth of his skin on mine, the taste of his soft lips, his groin, the tender backs of his knees.

His whimpers flooded my ears and made my balls tighten. His hole clenched at my probing tongue, and his sac firmed from my nuzzling.

And all the while, I ran my hands over him, smooth skin and wiry hair tickling my palms.

Mason was perfection. A divine treat for me to feast upon. And feast, I did.

"This was supposed to be about you," he gasped out as I slid a spit-slickened finger deep into his ass while licking up his taint.

"Loving on you *is* all about me—can't you tell how much pleasuring you gets me off?" I ground my hips, smearing pre-cum over his leg my dick pressed against.

"Looking at you...touching you, turns me on, baby." I kissed the tip of his hard length, sliding my tongue over his slit in search of his bitter flavor.

Grasping the base of his dick, I stroked upward while rubbing his prostate.

"Ah, fuck." Mason's back arched—and I got the bead of moisture I'd hoped for.

I lapped and suckled around his glans, swallowing the taste of him down.

"Jasper—I need you. Please."

Sliding my finger from his ass, I lowered my head. A slow lick up through his crack, all the way to the tip of his shaft sent a jolt through his body. "Want my dick, baby?"

"Yes."

"Are you going to take it all like a good boy?"

"*Fuck* yes."

The desperation in his voice brought a grin to my face, and with one last kiss to his belly, I scooted for his bedside table for supplies.

Face flushed and pupils blown, Mason watched my every move. The hunger rolled from him in undulating waves, attempting to pull me over. But a storm raged inside me too, swells of desire crashing against his in the space between us.

Panted breaths filled the air as I gave him two lubed fingers. His moan swirled eddies of lust low in my groin. A third finger bowed his back off the bed, and he hissed at me, writhing and grasping at his sheets.

"Your body is so hungry for me. Hot." I reached in deep, the base of my three fingers stretching him wide. "Silky smooth."

"Ung..." He swallowed hard. "Need you, Jasper."

My name had never sounded so sweet, so perfect on a

man's lips as it did on Mason's. That falling shit didn't touch the surface of how I felt.

Fuck my fantasies from childhood. I hoped to have Mason beside me for the rest of my life. Through the good and ugly. Fighting together, we would make ours the love of a lifetime.

Sliding my fingers from his heat, I sat back on my haunches and reached for the condom. I couldn't wait anymore. Needed to sink into him—be *one* with him.

"Can...can we go without?" Mason peered at me, his eyes hopeful.

Like him, I was on PrEP and had always used condoms. We'd discussed being negative but hadn't made a decision on continued rubber usage.

"You want me bare?" I asked, double-checking.

"I need to feel your cum leaking out of me."

Fuck.

My dick bucked in agreement. I tossed the foil packet aside and slid up over his body, widening my knees to catch hold of his thighs and lift them toward his chest. My length pressed against his taint, and I rubbed, smearing lube all over his groin.

Such exquisite friction...so damn slick and hot. "How about I unload right now and coat your dick and balls with my seed?"

Mason shuddered and gulped.

Smirking, I kissed his parted lips. "Definitely saving that one for another time." I reached between us and grabbed the base of my cock, teasing the head over his puckered hole. "You're going to take this dick."

"Yes."

"Every thick inch without complaint."

"Jesus, Jasper—yes. Please."

I pushed in, stretching him wide with one steady thrust.

Fingers dug into my back, and I swallowed down Mason's grunt as my balls came to settle against his ass. He'd admitted to loving girth, feeling spread open to the point of pain, so I didn't offer him time to adjust. I set a hard, relentless pace, giving him what he wanted. He shifted beneath me, grasping and holding me close, moaning over my tongue.

Our bodies crashed together, and I wished our souls could intertwine as easily as our panted exhales. I couldn't get deep enough. Couldn't bury myself to the point he would feel a literal piece of me inside him until he breathed his last.

Having Mason beneath me was exquisite torture, and I would gladly pay with my soul to fulfill his intense need.

"You're breaking me," he gasped out, eyes once more welling.

In this, I *could* put him back together. "I'm yours, Mase —and I'll always take care of you." My hips slammed into him, his hot body a welcoming refuge for my aching cock. "You feel so fucking good, baby."

I lifted onto my hands so I could see where I penetrated him. Slowing my thrusts, I angled upward with a gyrating roll to tag his sweet spot.

"Oh God." He gulped, pre-cum dripping from his rigid dick. "Right there."

"Here?" I repeated the motion, and his eyes rolled back.

"Fuck, yes."

I continued gliding into his heat, the slick lube creating a sexy squelching noise with every slow thrust. "Going to fill you up. Make a mess of you."

"Want you to breed me." He lifted his hips in perfect rhythm with my long, lingering strokes as though riding the same wave I did toward fulfillment. Mason chased, but I kept at a steady pace, loving on his hole and prostate with my dick, driving myself fucking wild in the process.

"Jasper," he moaned a pitiful plea for more.

I grasped my length on a backward glide, slicking up my palm and fingers with lube. "Going to make this so damn good for you, Mase. You'll cry when you come in my hand."

I palmed the head of his dick and slid my fist downward while rocking back into his ass.

"Fuck!" He arched beneath me, neck corded, lips parted.

"Yeah, baby...just like that," I murmured, my voice low and broken with breathlessness.

"Need...more, Jasper! Harder—please!"

"Nuh uh." I denied him, slow and steady in my drive to bring him to completion. "Want you to come just like this."

"C-Can't."

"You can." I tagged his prostate, milking his cock with my hand until pre-cum dripped onto his abs.

My arm holding my weight began to shake. Sweat dripped from my temples as I fought to keep in control with unhurried yet forceful thrusts.

"Need." Mason grasped my head and yanked me down. Our mouths collided.

He came, ropes of cum spurting between us, his hot ass rippling around my shaft with strangling force.

I couldn't hold back, couldn't wait until he finished. My balls tightened, and shots of release erupted where I buried inside him with a deep groan. "Fuck, baby." My hips stuttered, swiveled as he continued to clench around me. "So hot." I clasped his face, uncaring that his cum coating my hand, and ate at his mouth, needing oxygen, his exhales swirling in my lungs.

Our orgasms faded, and we panted together, our skin sticky and slick with sweat. My body burned, my thoughts shattered, and my emotions floated high above reality.

I wanted to linger there. Stay forever.

Mason seemed of the same mind, and neither of us made a move to sever the connection between us.

Chapter 19

Mason

Eventually, Jasper's cock softened and slipped from my body. His cum leaked from my sore hole, both of us finding great satisfaction in my feeling it. Him watching it.

"Hottest thing ever," Jasper declared, trailing fingertips through the stickiness over my swollen pucker. Kneeling between my spread thighs, he stared at my ass. "Look at that." He pressed a single finger inside me, and I hissed. "Fuck, that's the most erotic sight I've ever seen," he murmured.

His touch stung, but seeing the lust in his eyes when they'd been sated moments before tempted my dick to rouse. I grabbed hold of his shoulder, needing his mouth on mine.

Jasper laved over my torso, gathering up what remained of my spunk with his tongue. Most had smeared or dried between us, but enough lingered that I tasted myself on him when he licked into my mouth.

He settled his weight atop me, and we rubbed on one

another with lazy movements, no intentions other than intimacy. No endgame spurring us onward.

"Let me clean you up so we can rest, okay?"

I followed along like a sheep into the shower and allowed Jasper to wash my body. He kissed and caressed every inch of my skin once he finished. I tried to slip to my knees to show him my appreciation, but he wouldn't have it.

"Spoiling you pleasures me," he'd murmured against my lips, so I didn't argue.

One day, I told myself, Jasper would let me take the lead. Not that I had any desire to top him—we were in total agreement about our roles in the relationship—but I wanted to pamper him too.

Jasper passed out in bed before I did, and even though my window unit AC ran cool, the heat of our bodies entwined from head to toes became too much.

I eased from his hold and lay on my back, working through my emotions since my mind refused to rest.

Jasper's sweetness, his forgiving nature, seemed like a fairy tale. I wasn't sure I was worthy of his love. We hadn't used the L word, but I'd experienced the emotion he felt toward me when he moved inside me. Caressed me. Kissed me. All he did was *give* from beginning to completion every time we came together. I'd never met such a selfless man hellbent on showing me my worth.

I'd dreamed of being on the receiving end of a relationship for so long, but...

But.

Allowing him to love on me in the way he wanted was also a form of giving. I'd never thought it could be that way, beautiful and fulfilling—until Jasper.

If things had gone badly from the onset of our conversation, if he'd walked away...

I couldn't even think about it.

Shaking my head at the panic that attempted to rise inside me, I shifted to my side and retrieved my cell off my bedside table. It was after eleven, and even though Kellen had a client that night, I wanted to let him know that everything had turned out perfectly.

The message looked like a novel, but I poured the bulk of Jasper's and my exchange in one text and sent it off, not expecting a reply until morning.

My chest felt light. My heart at ease. Even my mind stayed quiet as I clasped my cell atop my chest, remembering how slowly Jasper had brought me to orgasm. Long, drawn-out strokes, pegging my prostate like a goddamned pro, his slick hand jacking me with a firm, sure grasp—

A ding pulled me from the edge of arousal, and I lifted my phone to find Kellen had replied.

Kellen: **I'm happy for you. So glad it went well.**

Me: **Are you off the clock?**

Kellen: **Yeah, thank fuck. Tonight was one of those clients where shit felt wrong from the start, you know? Uncomfortable. Stilted conversation.**

Me: **Ugh. Yeah, I hear you.**

Kellen: **The sex at the end was good at least. We both got off, and I left him satisfied. Job accomplished?**

I chuckled, having wondered the same quite a few times myself. **Was he a new client?**

Kellen: **Yep. Nervous as fuck, poor guy. Pretty sure my dick was the first he's had inside his**

ass, but rather than being stoked about it, I was…bored.

My brow furrowed.

Kellen: **Banging a different man just about every other night seemed like good payback once upon a time, but it's starting to get old.**

Kellen's ex-fiancé had cheated on him two days before their wedding, torn his heart in two, and left him to bleed out with a pile of debt for vows that had never gotten exchanged. His retaliation had been to become an Elite, and he'd had plenty of dick in his time with the company. I wondered over his lack of enthusiasm when he'd been driven to fuck as many men as he could without getting his heart involved.

Me: **What are you going to do?**

A few minutes of deep quiet passed as I waited for my friend to reply. Jasper still hadn't stirred from where he curled up beside me, hand resting beneath his smooth cheek.

He was so damn pretty. I barely refrained from running my fingertips over his nose, along his plump, lower lip I wanted to nibble on. In sleep, a natural blush stained his cheeks, and I imagined him wearing a pink shirt unbuttoned —and matching panties cradling his bulge.

Damn.

He would eventually share that part of him with me, but maybe I could drop hints that I wouldn't be turned off by him allowing his feminine side out to play. Let him know without saying a word about my snooping in his bottom drawer that I would accept him no matter what.

Give him anything he wanted, any time of the day.

A ding pulled my focus to my cell.

Kellen: **Maybe I ought to go back to Maine for good and finally lick my wounds rather than a bunch of random dicks.**

His wording caused a smirk to curl my lips. Kellen definitely enjoyed getting on his knees—offering his mouth as a *fuck you* to his ex. He held the power in making that choice, and no one but him could take it away.

Me: **I'm here if you want to talk it out. I'll help you pack, do whatever you need.**

Kellen: **I appreciate you, man.**

Me: **Same.**

Jasper shifted onto his back, and I once more gave him my full focus. His hair stuck up at all angles, his nose wrinkling as a frown flitted over his brow. Breath steady, his expression soon relaxed.

God, did I want him—so damn badly. I would willingly offer anything. Give *up* everything to keep him in my life forever.

Tapping my messaging app open once more, I clicked on Micah's name. My fingers didn't shake as I typed out my official resignation from Elite.

I probably should have waited to speak with him in person, but I realized after setting my cell aside and curling toward my lover that my body had needed complete closure before it would even consider rest.

Like all good things, peaceful sleep came to an end.

I dreamed of Joseph's deceitful smile. Blue eyes that lied. Hands that took—hurt—rather than soothed. He once more shook me to my core, ripping my calm away.

And in the moment between dreaming and waking, he fought against Jasper's pull on my mind.

Dark and light.

Fear and joy.

Assault and comfort.

Gentle kisses on my panting mouth drew me back to reality. Words promising loyalty and tender protection encouraged me to open my eyes.

Jasper leaned over me—not Joseph.

I buried my face in his chest and wept yet again, overrun by emotions. He held me without complaint, offering nothing but words to build me up and warm touches to help ground me.

Shutting down didn't exist as an option when I lay in Jasper's arms. He forced me to remain vulnerable. Open to distraction and redirection of my thoughts. And I loved him for choosing me. Believing in me. Wanting the best for my life.

I fell asleep once more, tangled in his arms, his steady heart beating beneath my ear, the heat of his skin against my cheek.

Jasper was my safe place, and I would face whatever hell was necessary in order to keep him.

Chapter 20

Jasper

The stars aligned for my lover, and days passed without any more nightmares creeping in to ruin Mason's sleep.

I went to work and came home sometimes to dinner and candlelight. Mason wasn't a chef by any means, but the effort he put into our meals warmed my heart. We cleaned up together regardless of who cooked, a deep friendship developing atop the physical connection we nurtured almost every night.

Mason suggested he ought to stay at his apartment after a week straight in my bed, but I wouldn't allow it. The idea of him not being beside me while sleeping brought about a discomfort I didn't care for one bit. He'd been meant to be by my side, and I wouldn't hear otherwise.

But it was too soon to insist he just pack up all his shit and move it into my place. We would get there though, probably sooner than later.

I brought Mason to Humanity House with me one morning to meet Zeke. My friend had agreed to have a session with him before office hours, and Mason had insisted I sit in with them. He'd claimed he had nothing to hide, that he wanted me to hear every memory, every thought in his mind so there would never be questions about his past nor miscommunication between us.

The three of us chuckled over that last bit, knowing full well there was no stopping things from being taken the wrong way or even coming out incorrectly. It was Mason's heart that mattered, so I agreed to join in with them on a weekly basis. The first had been a deep dive into his childhood, the manipulations of his mother, and their lack of contact once he'd moved out at twenty.

It had been Mason's suggestion to start from the beginning, rip the Band-Aid off, and get to the root of the matter. He had no wish to waste time in his drive to fix what he saw as broken.

But I found him to be as beautiful as he claimed I was. Every flaw, every sharp-edged piece, every scar—he belonged to me, and I adored him. Yes, he tended to be a slob, and I expected some days I would probably gripe about boxer briefs on the bathroom floor and damp towels not properly hung up on the drying rack, but the little stuff wouldn't change my intensifying attachment to him.

I studied the man sitting beside me, the strong profile of his nose and moving lips as he spoke to Zeke. We sat for our second session, my heart happy over how Mason's face revealed his true self. No mask covered his emotions, no veil shadowed his inner thoughts. He'd found a sense of freedom in my acceptance and a safe space with Zeke as well because of my trust in my friend.

Mason laid himself bare while clinging to my hand, and I felt beyond thankful for the opportunity to be with him and support him in his personal growth.

But mine? It had stalled out years earlier.

I was stuck in the mud, still hearing my dad's voice telling me how useless of a man-child I was. No matter my self-sacrificing, I'd never measured up, and I hated that he continued to control me from the grave.

I longed to break free. Be *me* in every sense—

"I've always been afraid to reveal myself," Mason said, his thumb stroking over the back of my hand, "but Jasper makes me *want* to be a better man."

Fuck, fuck, fuck.

My throat tightened, and I bit my tongue as I'd done throughout our first session with Zeke. Our meetings weren't about me and my issues, nor did I have a right to influence or guide Mason. This path he'd agreed to traverse allowed me to walk beside him, but in this, he led.

I hoped to help, prove myself useful to him beyond what he'd already claimed I'd done. Remaining silent hurt as much as the grief I experienced over the part of me I'd buried in order to keep Mason.

A few long minutes later, our time together ran out, and we left Zeke's office, heading down Humanity House's back corridor toward the rear exit.

"You were amazing today," I told Mason, squeezing his hand.

The smile on his face and the light in his eyes sent a sweet ache through my chest. He thrived beneath words of praise, and I gave them to him every chance I got.

"Thank you for staying with us again," Mason said. "It makes it easier to not hold back with Zeke."

"Anything for you, baby." I pushed open the heavy metal door that led to the employee parking lot. We'd both driven since I had work for the next eight hours, and Mason had an interview for the job opening with Silas's business. We ambled toward his car I'd helped him clean out, thrilled with how he fared in keeping the interior tidy due to that checklist I'd created for him on my own fridge.

"Good luck with your interview," I told him, taking him into my arms once we reached his vehicle. I pressed my lips to his temple, wanting to melt at how he nuzzled his whiskers into my neck and gently kissed me.

"Thanks," he murmured, his breath hot on my skin.

A shiver slid down my spine, lifting the hairs on my nape. I wasn't usually ticklish, but I would deal to enjoy just a few more precious seconds of his attention.

He stepped back way too soon, his eyes at rest. Happy.

"I'm proud of you, baby," said, cupping his cheek.

His eyelids closed, and he swallowed audibly.

"None of that." I removed my touch and slapped his ass. Hard. "Focus on your interview. This one won't be with Silas, but if you get called back for a second, it will. Troy told me the woman you're meeting with today, Shari, is a sweetheart—and I'll let you in on a little secret—she was married to an abusive narcissist for ten years before breaking free."

Having that tidbit of information would give Mason's subconscious some comfort when sitting with her.

Blowing out a steady exhale, Mason nodded. "I'm a good fit for the position on that team Silas is building. I'm just nervous."

"As anyone would be." I straightened his tie and smoothed down his starched collar even though it didn't need it. "Now go and nail this interview, and when I get home tonight, I'll allow you drop to your knees for me to celebrate."

Mason's pupils swelled, his lips parted. "You're finally going to let me give you something?"

"Mason." I pursed my lips and shook my head. We'd

had the discussion before about what he'd realized one night while not being able to sleep. Even though truth had clicked in his brain, sometimes he forgot how fulfilling my desire to love him was a gift he laid at my feet—or rather, on my bed. "You're the best at both—offering me your body and taking my cock. I couldn't ask for a better man."

His eyes welled, and I had to slap his ass again. "Get in your car, baby. And be yourself—let Shari know the real you because I promise—she's going to be impressed by who you are."

He drove away a few minutes later, and since I had roughly ten minutes before my office hours started, I headed on foot to the Dunks three blocks down from Humanity House. I shot off a text to see if Zeke wanted anything.

While the summer sun lay warm on my back as it rose in the sky, the heat of the day hadn't yet taken over the air. Thankful the nonprofit I worked for didn't require a strangling tie around my neck, I breathed deep, telling myself complete contentment and peace would eventually settle over me.

Mason and I had agreed to let our past remain behind us—I just had to focus on doing as he had been finding the strength to do. Perhaps it was time for me to return to therapy and find a way to move on from the part of me that could never again see the light of day.

The scent of coffee and donuts assaulted me as I stepped into Dunks, grinning that a star had aligned for me. I'd somehow hit a lull in their usual morning rush. I strode right up the counter and gave my and Zeke's orders, noting the sounds of others filing in the entrance behind me. While I'd already had waffles and strawberries with Mason earlier that morning, Zeke had skipped breakfast and had asked for a bacon, egg, and cheese on an onion bagel.

A hand brushed over my bare elbow, and I shifted to the side, smiling to offer apologies for bumping into the person behind me.

I recognized the blond curls, the sly smirk on his lips, but his blue eyes carried that same glint from the last time I'd run into him.

"Well, hello again, handsome," he purred, leaning toward me in a cloud of flowery perfume.

I stepped back fully, creating distance between us. "Good morning," I stated gruffly, needing to dismiss him and for the Dunks employee to get me Zeke's sandwich asap.

"Can I help you?" The worker behind the counter said to the blond, turning his focus off me.

"I'll just have one of those blueberry muffins, Janice," he spoke as though he knew the woman, his wink making her blush.

"You got it, Joseph."

The blood left my head on a crash course with my toes.

Blond. Dressed in a rose-colored top and designer jeans with a hint of a pink thong peeking from the waist band. Joseph.

Fuck.

I spun on my heel and walked out of Dunks without Zeke's sandwich, but I couldn't wait, couldn't take the chance of Joseph Delaney the third wanting to converse with me again. I feared smashing in his nose for what he'd done to Mason—for making it impossible for me to one day be free to dress like I truly wanted.

I also feared him pulling a knife to slash my face.

He'd stopped texting Mason, but the threats he'd made, the words he'd written, assured us the young man wasn't stable.

Had he followed me? Watched us in the parking lot?

"Hey!"

Flinching, I glanced over my shoulder.

Joseph hurried toward me, bag in hand. "You forgot your order!"

Swallowing hard, I forced my feet to remain still. Enough people littered the sidewalks around us that I didn't think he would attack me for breaking that supposed bond he had with Mason.

His smile didn't reach his eyes, but he didn't seem a threat while approaching and handing me Zeke's breakfast.

"Thanks," I rasped, taking care not to touch his hand in the exchange.

Joseph didn't speak. Just stared like a creep and allowed me to walk away without another word.

Goose bumps rose along my nape and arms, but I refused to look back in a show of concern of any sort.

Humanity House's rear heavy door slammed shut behind me, and I sagged against the solidity of metal, fighting to calm my racing heart.

As much as I wanted to believe Joseph appearing like that was pure circumstance, I couldn't. Same as the first time I'd run into him near Mason's apartment. The young man stalked him. Perhaps me.

Mason needed to be made aware—I had to tell him about the first encounter too now that I knew who the cherub-like young fucker was.

But it could wait.

Mason headed toward an interview for a job to replace the one he'd given up for me. Even though I expected he would have no problem nailing the interview, I couldn't risk sending his mind into a downward spiral.

I would tell him once I got home.

Chapter 21

Mason

I rode a high, pinching myself a few times to make sure reality didn't fuck with me.

I'd gotten the job. One interview that had included laughter and an ease of natural-flowing conversation, and Shari had offered me the position on the spot. I wondered if Troy had something to do with it, but I wasn't about to poke around and ask.

Micah hadn't been upset by my text that night telling him I was quitting Elite—he'd expected my resignation and had already told Preston I wasn't available when he'd called a few days earlier to book with me. I didn't ask if Preston had agreed to another Elite for the night but told Micah to give the young man my best wishes should he talk to him again.

While Preston had become somewhat of a friend, our relationship as it were lay in my past, as did any puzzle over who his stepbrother might be. I needed to focus on moving forward, forgetting everything behind me.

Micah asked about Joseph, but I'd told him that things had calmed down. There'd been no texting or calls, so I was hopeful shit had run its course. Perhaps Joseph had found a real sugar daddy. He hadn't booked with Elite again, not that Micah would have allowed him to anyway.

Excitement for my future hit me like it never had before. Things looked up. *Way* up.

My need for Jasper by my side hadn't changed one bit. I would never get enough of him, but with his support, I'd become more confident and successful in daily living. And speaking with Zeke, unloading everything I'd kept bottled up inside me for so long was cathartic.

I felt lighter. Peace I'd never expected filled me completely, and my outlook on life finally held meaning.

Climbing into my car encased me in stifling heat, but I just ripped off my tie and got the AC cranking. A wide grin on my face, I powered up my cell to let Jasper know the good news.

An unknown number had texted me since I'd blocked the last one, but the first line left no question as to the sender.

It was an image of Jasper holding me outside Humanity House earlier in the morning.

Unknown Number: **If you think you can replace me with sweet little Jasper, you're sorely mistaken.**

Unknown Number: **I tried to do the same with another sugar daddy, but no one else will ever hold my heart. I had to let that guy go.**

Unknown Number: **No one will ever fill my boy pussy the way you do either. They all fall short.**

Unknown Number: **I want you and your dick again, and there's nothing I won't do to have you. Keep you forever.**

Sweat broke out over my body as my heart thrummed. Stomach twisting to the point of physical pain, I stared at the messages. My smile had dissolved, all traces of happiness gone in a flash. Floundering didn't begin to describe my soul.

I rang Jasper's cell, and it went straight to voice mail.

"Fuck!" Shaking, I attempted to call Humanity House direct but misdialed three times before connecting.

"I-I need to talk to Jasper," I gasped out when the secretary answered.

"I'm sorry, he's in a meeting at the moment. Can I take a message?"

"No—I have to speak to him now. It's an emergency." My voice edged on hysteria.

"Can I ask who's calling, please?"

"Mason. His boyfriend."

"Oh, hi, Mason! I've heard so much about you!" Her evident joy would have been welcome five minutes earlier.

"Jasper," choked on his name, my mind ready to tumble into lockdown mode. "N-Need him."

"Okay...can you hold on for just a minute?" Concern bled through the line as though she'd picked up on my anxiety, and I managed to whisper an affirmative.

It took longer than sixty seconds—I counted while waiting. By two hundred, my lungs began to close off. At three hundred, I struggled for breath, going light-headed.

"Mason?"

Jasper.

I couldn't say his name, but I managed to make a noise so he knew I was there.

"Mason, what's going on? Where are you?"

"C-Can't breathe." I managed to gasp out the two words.

"Baby—I need you to listen to me. I'm here, and I can hear you. You're going to be all right—I promise." His voice alone calmed me enough I got a sip of oxygen into my lungs. "You're going to follow my directions, okay?" Jasper asked, and I nodded, only half-aware he couldn't see me. He began counting, telling me when to inhale and exhale.

With every second that passed, my closed eyes and mind focused on the sound of his voice that brought me away from the edge of falling under. His control, his calm tone when telling me I was doing such a good job swept through my thoughts, wrapping them up in a comfortable hold.

Restricted lungs relaxed, and I eventually inhaled on my own.

"I-I'm alright," I finally told him, less terrified but far from the high I'd been on while walking out of Silas's building.

"What happened, baby?"

"I got the job."

"Damn!" Jasper laughed as though relieved. "That's amazing, Mason! I'm so proud of you."

"Thanks." I sagged onto my driver seat, tipping back my head as though I had zero energy left in my body.

"Is that why you had an anxiety attack?" He'd figured it out without my explaining—had known exactly what I'd needed.

God, did I love him.

Tears stung my eyes, and I swallowed down a sob.

"Mase?"

"He's at it again," I whispered.

"Joseph?" Jasper asked, his tone wary.

"Yes."

"What did he do?"

I swiped a forearm over my wet eyes. "More texts."

"Shit. Where are you?" Jasper clipped his words.

"Sitting outside of Silas's office building. I turned on my cell to text you that I got the job, and a couple of messages waited for me. He took a picture of us, Jasper." I shuddered, my heart rate picking up again. "He was watching us hug this morning and told me he would do whatever it took to get me back."

"We have to go to the courthouse and file that harassment order right now, Mason," Jasper stated, his tone as unsteady as I felt.

As much as I wanted what he'd said—*we*—I knew I should do it without him holding my hand.

"I don't need you to go with me. I've got this," I assured him, only a little confident in myself. I couldn't hang on his coattails for everything. "Besides, you're in that meeting with the board. I'll be fine on my own."

Jasper exhaled slowly. "Okay. Call me if there's an emergency."

I forced a lightness to my voice. "I will." He would be safe at Humanity House. Joseph wouldn't touch him. At least, I hoped not. "And do me a favor?" I tacked on. "Don't go outside alone. Have Zeke walk you to your car at the end of the day. Just in case."

"I will," Jasper said. "Promise."

Feeling somewhat calmed, I hung up.

The drive north on Route 1 was agonizing yet numbing at the same time. I held the steering wheel in autopilot, a fog of worry pulling my focus inward rather than on the road. My subconscious took me toward Peabody since my thoughts settled on the texts and what Joseph had been up to earlier that morning. He didn't live in Malden, would have no reason to be hanging outside Humanity House unless he'd been literally stalking me.

Did he follow me still?

I glanced in my rearview, dozens of cars in my line of sight. With no clue what kind of vehicle Joseph drove, I wasted my time. What if he'd put a tracker on my car? It wouldn't surprise me if he had access to those sorts of things with his bank account. Maybe he'd somehow hacked into my phone while I'd been passed out from his drugs, and he could listen in on all my conversations.

Did he wait for me at the courthouse? Would he jump me once I parked?

A million other scenarios started rushing through my head—needles stabbed into my neck. Getting dragged into a dark van. Being tied down once more to his bed.

My heart began to race again—I couldn't call Jasper. *Wouldn't.*

"You've got this," I whispered to myself, pushing against the fear rising to choke me.

I didn't.

I couldn't have my lover for what I faced, but I had a loyal friend.

"Hey, Siri—call Kellen," I spoke at my cell, my voice shaky as fuck.

"What's up, Mason?" he answered a few seconds later.

A relieved sigh rushed from my lungs, and I loosened my hold on my steering wheel from its death grip. "Are you busy?"

"Not until later tonight."

"Can I borrow your muscles and potent scowl for an hour or two?"

After explaining what had gone down that morning,

Kellen was more than happy to meet me at the courthouse and act as my bodyguard.

I hung up and debated texting Jasper to let him know I wouldn't be alone. It wasn't pertinent information, nor was it an emergency, so I decided against it. Best to allow my man finish his meeting in peace, and I could fill him in once we finished.

Hopefully, the paperwork wouldn't take long to file, and Joseph would leave us both the hell alone.

Chapter 22

Jasper

I couldn't concentrate worth a shit.

The board discussed the midyear updates and reports a month late due to two of the members being overseas since early July. We didn't have much to hash out, but a few members looked through papers with fine-tooth combs, painstakingly slow. Thorough to the point their anal retentiveness needed a damn enema.

Or perhaps, for the first time since being hired to oversee Humanity House's daily operations, my priorities focused elsewhere.

Mason hadn't wanted me to go with him to the courthouse. He'd sounded almost...flippant in brushing aside my suggestion we head over there together to file the harassment order. Didn't he know I would drop everything at a moment's notice for him? Work, family...nothing meant more to me than him and his well-being.

He'd said he could do it on his own.

The reminder tightened the vise around my chest I'd been struggling with since hanging up with him and returning to the meeting a half hour earlier. Sips of water didn't help take my mind off feeling useless. Clearing my throat only earned me a few glances from those around the table.

I could sense Zeke's stare from his seat beside me.

Did he notice my hands clenched on my lap to keep from fiddling due to the churning in my stomach? Had my bouncing knee caught his eye? Was my shifting backside disturbing enough I gave my anxious state away?

Fuck.

Swallowing hard, I closed my eyes. My palms grew damp, my pulse speeding.

I'd never had a panic attack—was that what rose inside me? That sense of being out of control, powerlessness? I hated not being in charge of my emotions or anything else when it pertained to my personal life.

I fucking floundered because my lover had gotten through his own stress, then declared he could take care of business himself.

He no longer needed me.

Once he accomplished his task at the courthouse, would he realize he easily *could* stand on his own two feet without a hand to hold? Would he no longer see me as his rock, his post to lean on? Would the connection, that fulfillment of our emotional needs we'd found with one another, unravel at his independence and the sudden confidence he found?

"Jasper," Zeke whispered, touching my forearm and jerking my eyelids open.

I shook my head, too worked up to answer.

"Hey, guys...mind if we take a little coffee break?" Zeke asked. A few voices murmured their agreement, and he clasped my shoulder as others climbed from their chairs. "Let's go."

Like a marionette, I moved with his hand grasping my

arm to my feet. Away from the table we'd sat around. Out the conference room's door.

He led me to my office down the back hallway before speaking a word. "Sit."

I collapsed in the nearest chair, the one across from my desk as he closed the door, giving us privacy.

Zeke dragged the other seat beside mine closer, spun it around to face me, and perched on its edge. Concern etched in his brow as he shifted forward, elbows on his knees. "What's going on?"

I'd already explained to him about Joseph at Dunks earlier that morning when giving him his breakfast. I'd also leaned close to him after returning from Mason's phone call to let him know who'd been behind our secretary pulling me from the room. But I hadn't been able to share the whole story or ask him for help in directing my scattered thoughts in that moment.

I should have—I wouldn't have spiraled nearly as bad as I did.

"Joseph is texting him again. I told Mason I would go to the courthouse with him and file the harassment order." I swallowed hard. "He...he said he didn't *need* me."

Zeke didn't normally crack his counselor's calm façade, but a hint of a smirk curled his lips. "He's finally showing a bit of confidence in himself, and you get all unsure in your relationship? Jasper." Zeke shook his head. "I'm not invalidating your feelings, but this is a *good* thing. Healthy. It's exactly what you've been hoping for, isn't it?"

Cursing, I tipped my head back, eyelids slamming shut. "I've never felt this way for a man before—the power he holds over me...I'm acting insecure as fuck. And what he did makes me think I'm no longer necessary, you know?" My voice broke, and I swallowed hard.

Zeke knew about my father and how he'd treated his "useless faggot son", but I'd kept what had brought on that conversation in my childhood from Zeke. It was bad enough he was aware of the kind of bullying I'd endured as a kid. The man didn't need to know the horrific details of what Mason had endured that doubled down my need to be a "real man" as my father had often said.

Zeke chuckled and clasped my knee, giving it a friendly squeeze. "Mason adores you. Even if he had a backbone of steel and enough confidence for ten men, he would still need you, my friend. Trust me. He looks at you like Levi does with me. Mason would lay down his life, face fifty Josephs, in order to be with you."

A huge exhale flattened my lungs, and I sagged. Adrenaline crashes sucked ass. "I feel like I'm going to puke," I muttered. Another snicker left Zeke, and I glared at him. "It's not funny."

"I understand the agonizing wondering, the not knowing, of being on unsteady ground in a relationship that hasn't been clearly defined. It was the same for me until Levi showed up at my parents' that Sunday afternoon, and we clarified what we both hoped for. The future both of us had dreamed about. Eventually, we made it happen."

Zeke patted my knee and sat back in his chair. "Confidence comes with communication. Tell Mason exactly what you're feeling—that you're far beyond falling, that you want more than just being boyfriends. Explain how you're hoping for forever with him."

"I do."

"You *both* do. I've experienced that kind of bond and can spot it a mile away. Even before I met Mason, I knew you were a goner. Look at what you're feeling like this: being the caretaker in a relationship sometimes means letting the other stretch their wings and realize they can fly alone. The beauty is that men like Mason don't *want* the independence for long. He'll come back to you—you're his home. His safe place."

How many times had Mason stated those exact words to me? They had flooded me with contentment, but I'd never taken his meaning to heart. I hadn't allowed his claims to give me what he'd planned—assurance of how he felt for me.

Mason had emotionally bared himself fully, but did I offer him the same in return? Did I vocalize anything he would see as a desire for permanence? I thought we had when talking about walking into our future together, but perhaps he hadn't read into the words as deeply as I did.

I definitely kept a part of myself from him—but no matter our connection, the bond we'd begun strengthening —I had to continue to stifle my deepest desires in order for our relationship's survival.

"Moments of him standing on his own two feet doesn't mean a breakup looms in your future," Zeke continued. "The way he clings to your hand, the things he says about you—you're stuck with that man for the rest of your life. I would bet my marriage on it."

Stuck. I huffed a laugh. More like blessed—same as Zeke with his husband.

"Thank you for reminding me of those truths," I murmured. "And also for pulling me out of there before I had a mental breakdown and embarrassed myself."

"Not a problem. Now, come on. Let's get this shitty meeting over with so we can go back to work then head home to our men."

A quick nod, and I stood, still slightly antsy, shaky from the aftereffects of skating the edge of a panic attack.

I had to trust Mason with his task, believe in him like I'd told him countless times I did. He was stronger than he claimed.

He does *have this.*

If only I could finish up the rest of my workday with the same confidence. Mason made me feel weak in a way I'd never experienced before, and while I didn't exactly like it, I could appreciate the reason for my worry.

I loved Mason Thomson. Wholeheartedly. Unconditionally.

If having his back meant standing in place while he stepped from beneath the umbrella of my protection, I would do so.

Even if it stirred up old wounds and hurt like hell.

Chapter 23

Mason

Kellen called me to let me know he'd arrived and had found parking on Railroad Ave. He told me to stay on speaker phone with him until I found him.

He leaned against the side of his SUV, cell to his ear when I turned onto the road and caught sight of him. Luckily, a spot sat empty a few slots down from him. I pulled in, some of the tension riding my shoulders releasing.

While Kellen looked like a suave model in his usual black attire, his scowl could intimidate the most confident of men. His ex had helped him hone that trait.

He kept a watchful eye as I shut off my car and climbed out, scanning everyone around us. "You okay?" he asked once seemingly satisfied that I hadn't been followed.

"I will be," I stated, "as soon as I get this figured out, then go home."

"Your place or Jasper's?" Kellen asked as we fell into step toward the courthouse on the corner.

Warmth rushed through at the realization I'd thought of

Jasper's place. "His," I said, my face heating, "but *he's* my home."

Kellen slung an arm around my shoulders for a quick bro hug. "I'm jealous, man. Seriously. From what you've said, he seems like a great guy. Perfect for you in every way."

"He really is."

A grin stretched my lips as we went into the courthouse, and it stayed in place while filing out the necessary forms. It took a little over an hour, but I submitted the information with the request Joseph not be made aware of the filing, which Troy had told me was possible.

An initial hearing would happen with a judge who would decide to give me the order or not. If so, the police would then serve papers to Joseph, and we would have to meet before the judge again to offer Joseph a chance to defend himself.

No charges—no criminal case. Simply a means of keeping him out of my life.

Feeling as though a weight had lifted off my chest, I followed Kellen outside and down the wide set of stairs.

"Mr. Thomson?"

I halted and turned.

Detective Jenner hurried toward us. "Mason," he said, coming up to me with his hand outstretched.

"Detective," I greeted. "What are you doing here?"

"Court." He glanced at Kellen who sidled up to me. Appreciation flared in his eyes as he took in a quick once-over of my friend from head to toe. Was the man gay, or did he always check out whoever approached his personal space with quick scrutiny? It was probably a law enforcement thing. "Do you have a minute?" he asked, giving me his focus.

"Sure."

Detective Jenner motioned with his head, away from the pathway of those going in and out of the courthouse. Tucked somewhat behind a bush, he turned toward me, once more eying Kellen at my side.

"He stays," I stated firmly.

The detective nodded. "I'm wondering if your thoughts on pressing charges has changed."

"It hasn't—I just filed a harassment order against him instead."

"Has he been in contact with you?"

I nodded. "Texts—outright threats on my life. Different number than the first time but the same shit."

A muscle ticked in Detective Jenner's smooth-shaven jaw. "You aren't the only man he's attacked," he stated quietly, glancing around as though checking to make sure no one listened in.

"What?" I shot out, my forehead furrowing.

"There was a similar incident...a couple of nights ago." Detective Jenner glanced at my chest. "The man was around your age. Drugged, same means of binding, but a different knife. That boy definitely has a type."

"Oh fuck."

"But unlike you, Joseph's latest victim wasn't employed by Elite." His gaze flitted to Kellen.

I shifted on my feet, but Kellen didn't flinch beneath the detective's knowing gaze.

"Look—I don't give a shit what the two of you do to make a living," Detective Jenner said, confirming my suspicion he was aware Kellen worked for Micah too. "My mom turned tricks to keep food on our table when I was little. People do what they have to in order to survive. You'll get no judgment from me."

"H-How did you find out?" I asked.

"You said you'd been in the Sweet Water Suite on the night of the attack. The room had been rented by Jasmine Fox—Micah Fox's wife—for his fortieth birthday party. Simply looking into who he is revealed his lucrative business. You're both on his website's list of available escorts."

"I quit," I stated, lifting my chin.

"Like I said—I don't give a shit what you do," he repeated.

Kellen didn't offer any information, simply stood silent. Unmoved, arms crossed over his thick chest.

"So are you going to be able to get him for attempted murder or something with the other guy's case?" I asked.

"I can't discuss the charges at this time, but if you agreed to come forward with your story..."

"Maybe the other victim just needs a better lawyer?" I tossed out the first thought that came to mind. "Does he? I know people with the kind of money who could bury Joseph."

The detective smothered what sounded like a laugh wanting to escape. "The district attorney will be in charge of the case against Delaney, but yeah, you do have friends with deep pockets—so does that boyfriend of yours."

I shifted on suddenly restless feet. How much digging had the detective done into our lives?

Detective Jenner glanced at Kellen. "You're a good friend, Kellen Roberts."

Kellen took his time checking out the detective. "It seems like you're decent at your job, Detective..." He lifted a single eyebrow and waited.

"James Jenner." The detective offered his hand. "My friends call me JJ."

I side-eyed Kellen as the two men shook, their grasp on each other lingering as they stood eye to eye. There was no need for that gay radar thing. JJ found my bi friend hot as fuck.

Biting back a smirk, I elbowed Kellen.

The two men dropped their hands to their sides, both curling into fists as though wanting to hold onto the feel of the other. My heart might have melted a little bit.

"Mr. Thomson," the detective said, turning toward me.

"Mason," I reminded him. I had a feeling I might be calling him JJ again.

"Mason," he agreed with a nod. "Reconsider—two against one, double the evidence, will put that blond punk where he belongs. Behind bars for a long fucking time."

I nodded, already knowing I wouldn't involve myself further. Jasper and I had started a life together, and I was done with speed bumps. But first...

"How long until you have him in custody?" I asked, clueless to how warrants and all that shit worked, same as the entire court system and everything law.

A slow smile lifted the detective's mouth. "Sooner than later. I wouldn't be too worried crawling into bed tonight. He'll have his cell phone taken away and only be allowed one call. I'm sure that will be daddy dearest."

"Gotcha."

"Kellen." He dipped his head at my friend and spun on his heel, striding off.

I watched Kellen stare after him. "Hey." My elbow to his side again jerked his focus to me.

"What?"

"He's kind of hot," I tossed out to gauge his reaction.

Kellen's gaze flicked back toward the detective.

"And I'm not the greatest when it comes to reading people, but that JJ nickname offer? *And* the fact he doesn't give a shit you're an escort? Weren't you just saying the other day that you were...bored with boning strangers?"

Huffing, Kellen turned away and shook his head. "I don't do relationships. I had my shot—my one chance with true love. You know how that ended."

"Maybe you need to give yourself a *second* chance at finding your soulmate."

"Don't believe in that shit, either," he muttered, starting toward Railroad Ave. "Don't you have a boyfriend to get to?"

The thought of seeing Jasper and telling him everything that had gone down since I'd spoken to him earlier set my heart to racing again.

But in the best way possible.

That high I'd been on what seemed hours earlier? It didn't compare to how my heart soared.

Joseph Delaney had taken shit too far with another man who wouldn't be cowed, and his actions were going to bite him in the ass. I couldn't wait to hear all about it.

First, though, I had a worried lover in need of some good news—and a suckable dick to help celebrate how the day would end.

With Joseph in police custody.

And me, finally free of worry and ready to move onward with my new job and life with my forever man.

Chapter 24

Jasper

Only an hour remained until quitting time, and Zeke sat in my office with me, discussing an incident that had taken place between two teens not long after the board meeting had ended. Fists had flown, enough to bruise knuckles and make noses bleed. I expected two black eyes in twenty-four hours.

They'd both been sat down, read the riot act, and given tasks around the place for punishment. The janitors would welcome the two teens into their fold for the rest of the week's work.

At least the on-again/off-again friends had cleared the air between them on their own before an hour had passed. That didn't get them out of spending a few mornings with the cleaning staff though.

I glanced at my cell atop my desk. It sat silent. How long did it take to fill out paperwork and file a harassment order? Why hadn't he texted me with an update?

I swiped my cell to life to make sure—yet again—that I hadn't missed a notification.

"Go home," Zeke said, chuckling.

"Shut up," I muttered.

"Shit's done here for the day," Zeke stated, slapping my desk and rising to his feet. "Text your man to let him know you're leaving the office, pack up, and head out. It's been a long-as-fuck afternoon. If I'm beat and ready for my bed, I can imagine you're twice as drained."

"Seriously." I heaved a sigh, dragging my ass off my chair to gather my things as Zeke made for my door.

He opened it. "Oh—hey," I heard him say, sounding startled.

I glanced up.

Mason stood in front of Zeke, hand raised as though to knock. Pink flushed his cheeks as he glanced around my friend.

Our gazes connected, and my heart hit the goddamn floor before sprinting with rapid beats at his smile. Did time slow, or was that a figment of my imagination? I'd never seen Mason's face so full of happiness, and I'd never caught sight of the wrinkles around his eyes from a full-on grin either.

My boyfriend was fucking gorgeous.

My dick thoroughly agreed, swiftly swelling with the need to show him how much I loved him.

"Okay, then." Zeke cleared his throat while glancing between us. "I'll just see myself out." He stepped around Mason. "Have fun!" he called, disappearing down the hallway.

"Get your fine ass in here." I growled the words since Mason's expression said all I needed to know—things had gone well at the courthouse.

Mason scooted forward.

"Shut the door," I hastened to add. "And flip the lock."

He stuttered to a stop and spun back to obey my order.

Turning once more, he paused, studying me from where I stood unmoving behind my desk. Less than fifteen feet separated us, but it felt like a goddamn mile.

"Come here, baby," I held out my hand, getting off on how he rushed to listen to me—trusted me enough to submit to my every whim.

Mason slid his palm along mine, and I tugged him in fully against me. Hard muscle aligned with my body, and a shudder ripped through me as my dick made contact with his thigh, his against my lower stomach.

This man...

He shivered along with me, his lips quirking as though he struggled to keep quiet.

"Tell me."

"I'm so worked up right now," he said, his word rushed and breathless.

Lust shot through my cock, thickening me fully inside my pants. "I can see that," I said with a smirk and slid my hands around his waist to fill my palms with his juicy ass. Something good had my lover on a natural high. Definitely worthy of commemorating with an exchange of bodily fluids.

Mason clutched at the back of my shirt, shifting on his feet. "Detective Jenner was at the courthouse, and I talked to him. Joseph hurt another man like he did me—he's pressing charges and has a good case."

"Oh shit." Relief swept in, erasing the fear I'd had earlier in the morning thanks to Joseph's stalking us.

"Detective Jenner suggested that Joseph would be in cuffs before night's end—"

I cut Mason's words off, my mouth too desperate for a taste of him to hear anything else. There was nothing more to add in my opinion. All that mattered was Joseph would no longer be a threat to either of us.

We were free to move on without him to find our version of happily ever after—even if it didn't involve my secret desire to wear pretty things.

"I love you," I gasped out against Mason's mouth, needing him to understand fully where my heart was. "I believe in you, in us. I want forever with you, Mase." I pulled away from his addictive lips, studying his blown pupils, and the light, the goddamn *joy*, radiating from them was too damn much to comprehend.

"I love you, Jasper. The thought of not having you in my life makes me itchy to jump off a bridge. Sorry." Mason shook his head quickly. "Not really *jump*, jump, but you know what I mean."

"You can't stand the idea of living without me. I feel the same." Our foreheads tipped together.

"I-I think I have from the very beginning," Mason stated, his sweet breath caressing my mouth. "In one night, you took my heart."

"I didn't *take* it," I argued. "You gave it up to me on a platter."

"Then you'd best gorge on it. Or any other body part you want."

Chuckling at Mason's suggestive tone, I nipped his lower lip then sucked away the sting. "I need it all."

"I'm yours," he whispered.

"Damn right, you are."

Our kiss grew hungry, heads angling to deepen the touch, the intimacy between us. No one turned me on like my Mason. Never had a man filled me up inside like him. I could feel forever in every swipe of his tongue along mine, in how his hands continued to grasp my shirt and hold on as though I was his only hope of making his way through life.

I knew better though. He was strong and would only grow in self-confidence as our relationship blossomed. Holding still to let him be independent from my desire to protect him wouldn't get any easier, I expected, but my love for him would strengthen with every passing year. I would make use of every chance I could to show him. Tell him.

"On your knees, baby," I murmured into his mouth.

He dropped down without hesitation, going straight for my belt.

Chuckling, I grabbed his hair to tip his head back. So damn greedy for me.

His eager hands stilled as our gazes connected.

"You are so fucking perfect for me, Mason. I couldn't ask for a better man."

Wetness welled in his eyes, and he swallowed hard, his Adam's apple bobbing. "I love you."

"Show me how much." I loosened my grasp on his hair and caressed through the strands.

Mason had my pants to my knees within seconds, and he took me into his throat in one go.

"Fuck!" I hollered and bit my lip as he swallowed around my glans. "Holy fucking shit, Mase."

Forget not pulling his hair. I double-fisted, holding on for dear life as my lover worked me over. Sloppy as fuck, he sucked and licked. Nuzzled and nibbled. Fucking teased around my slit until I couldn't help but thrust over his tongue.

"Shit...your mouth is so hot."

Why the fuck had I insisted on waiting to give him my dick like this?

He gagged as I stabbed deep into his throat, but he kept

at it, drool dribbling. His hands found my ass, and he encouraged me to fuck his face.

I shoved in deep, and he groaned when I allowed him breath. "This what you want?" Another thrust earned me that beautiful gagging sound that caused the base of my spine to tingle.

"Mmm," he moaned around my girth, licking as I pulled out.

I shoved back in, and he whimpered. "Such a good boy taking my cock—so damn gorgeous. Fuck, you're going to make me come."

Another noise that sounded like a plea cut off as my dick disappeared into his mouth.

"Want my cum?"

"Mmm."

"Gonna swallow it all down then let me taste myself on your tongue?"

Eyes clenched shut, Mason shuddered—and I came like a geyser, shooting my load straight down his throat.

"Fuck yes—Mason. Oh my God, you're so good for me. So. *Fucking*. Good."

I trembled and yanked him to his feet. He melted into me as though spent, the bitterness of my cum on his lips and tongue. I dove in deep, needing to taste myself on him.

"Love you," I gasped, my pulse throbbing throughout my body as I rode the high of my orgasm.

He shivered and sighed as though he'd never been more content. From blowing me.

I grabbed hold of his ass and squeezed. "Want me to get you off now or tonight in our bed?"

Mason snickered and rubbed his whiskers over my neck. "I came in my pants like a teenage kid."

Why was that so damn hot? Guess my baby loved

sucking my cock as much as when I tagged his sweet spot with relentless strokes.

"That sounds uncomfortable," I murmured with a grin.

He snorted. "You have no idea."

"Been there. Done that—but a long time ago."

Pink flushed Mason's face when I cradled his head in my hands and pulled him back so I could better see him. "My beautiful, sweet man. Let's go home."

Chapter 25

Mason

We sprawled on our bed, sweaty and sated. My cell had dinged a half-dozen times while Jasper had been balls deep in my ass, but I'd ignored it. I still rode a high from knowing Joseph was undoubtedly in handcuffs or sitting in jail by now.

Darkness had fallen, and even though we needed a shower desperately before passing out, neither of us rolled to get off the rumpled, messy sheets. Cum dripped from my hole, and I rubbed absently at my chest.

Another text notification came through, and Jasper groaned from where he plastered his sweaty body to my back. "Gonna finally check your messages?" he mumbled, sounding half asleep.

"No."

Snickering, he stretched over my sprawled form to grab my cell from the bedstand. "The fuck..."

I blinked open my eyes, shifting onto my side as Jasper sat upright, eyes hard as he stared at my phone's screen. "What?"

"Fucker is still on the loose—"

Another text dinged.

"Fuck!" Jasper hopped up and, butt naked, rushed into the living room.

My heart kicked into high gear, and I stumbled from the bedroom.

Jasper stood near the window, peeking around the blind. "He's here—fucking *here*!"

Shit. Every muscle in my body froze.

"Goddamnit!" Jasper's hands shook as he fumbled with my phone, dialing. "Go get clothes on! Now, Mason!" he demanded, his tone low but urgent.

"911, what's your emergency?" I barely made out the operator pick up in the sudden stillness of Jasper's house.

Jasper's voice became a buzz in my ears as my brain started to shut down.

Couldn't. Function.

Joseph—should be in jail. How... Why was he outside? What had he texted?

"Mason!"

I blinked to find Jasper directly in front of me.

"Police are on their way. We have to get dressed."

Nodding dumbly, I stumbled back toward his room, his hand a vise grip around my wrist. He released his hold on me and grabbed his white briefs from off the floor and sweats from his bottom drawer. I fumbled to pull on my own pants.

He rushed back into the living room, leaving me alone. I struggled to put on a T-shirt, my breaths coming too fast. My legs went weak as I poked my head through the shirt, sliding my arms through the right holes.

A fist pounded on the front door.

Oh fuck. I gulped, once more frozen.

"Mason!" a voice shrieked, and although muffled by

doors and walls, I recognized its owner. "If you don't open this door right fucking now, I'll torch the place! You hear me! I fucking burn you and your pretty whore to ash!"

His words were slurred, but the threat hit me all the same.

I sank to the floor, curled into a ball.

Sirens rose in the distance, quickly overtaking the profanities spewing from Joseph's lips as he continued to rant.

The front door banged inward—Joseph's words cut off.

I whimpered, eyes clenched shut, shoving my fingers into my ears.

Muffled shouts sounded, but a keening welled inside my chest and erupted, blocking their words.

No, no, no...

"Mason!"

Jasper.

I cracked an eyelid to find him crouched beside me. Unharmed. His eyes full of relief.

"Cops are here, baby." He held out his arms, and I threw myself at him, sending us both against the wall. He shifted me sideways on his lap, and I clung to him, my face buried in his neck.

"Do you know who I am?!" Joseph's shrieks echoed through the house. "You're touching me without my consent!" he screamed—and I burst into manic laughter at the irony.

"You're under arrest—"

"No! I'll have your goddamn badges for this! You can't do this to me!" Joseph attempted to cut off the cop reading his rights, but the low tone continued on, slowly fading as they must have dragged Joseph outside.

Although lights flashed through the house's darkness, quiet settled briefly around us.

"Okay, Mase?"

I realized I still laughed, and I pushed away from Jasper's hold to wipe tears from my eyes. "Fuck—I can't even process right now. You...did you let that psycho in?"

"I didn't want him taking off before the police got here, and once I saw their lights, yeah. I opened the door and put a fist into his nose before he could blink."

More laughter rolled from me as the adrenaline crash of the century owned my muscles. "My God. I'm losing it."

Jasper smoothed my hair from my forehead, his soft smile bringing a trickle of calm through my fucked up nerves and the intense release of emotions.

"Mason?" Another voice I recognized called through the house.

"In here, detective!" Jasper hollered back.

JJ.

The high that had been cranking through me suddenly vanished, leaving me weak and shaky. I sank once more into Jasper and held onto him for dear life.

The news broadcasted Joseph appearing in court the morning after showing up at Jasper's front door, but he looked like a wrinkled mess rather than runway ready like I'd always seen him. Blond curls a disaster and dark smudges beneath his eyes with a hint of purple thanks to Jasper's fist, he'd stared at the judge with an arrogance of someone twice his age.

During the arraignment, he'd pled not guilty to drugging for sexual intercourse and aggravated rape among lesser charges.

His last name and father's money didn't keep the judge from denying him bail.

Jasper and I hadn't gotten much sleep thanks to having the cops all up in our space for hours on end. We'd learned the warrant had been issued for his arrest, but Detective Jenner hadn't been able to locate the little fucker until Jasper's 911 call.

After watching Joseph's face crumple at not being allowed freedom until his day in court? I slept like a baby and continued to do so knowing he had no access to me, Jasper, or a phone for the foreseeable future.

Five weeks after Joseph's arrest, my lover and I collapsed onto our bed after a long day of lugging boxes from my apartment to his house. I'd officially moved in with my boyfriend—my partner. The man who looked after me in every way.

A new chore chart hung on the refrigerator, and although I no longer needed the help in keeping my brain organized due to less emotional stress in my life, I enjoyed the structure. Pleasure filled me whenever I put a mark of completion in a box that Jasper had lovingly created for me, my favorites being sharing with him something personal about my day at work and edifying myself with a positive word.

Somedays, I felt self-sufficient but allowed him to pamper me by picking out my clothes and helping me dress. I adored standing in front of him, studying how his brow furrowed slightly while he knotted my tie. The brush of his knuckles on my skin, the soft pat to my chest once he finished, sent need tingling through me. Gentle kisses always followed, murmurs of his love to see me through our hours apart.

And my favorite moments awaited me in the evenings when Jasper reversed the process, stripping me down to my skin and worshiping my body with fingertips, tongue, and lips. He left me sated and claimed he found fulfillment in pleasuring me every single time.

I came to recognize that "savior" wasn't an exact fit for what Jasper had been for me but more a helpmate to encourage me in my personal growth. Meeting with Zeke on a weekly basis, sometimes without Jasper, shifted my mind toward emotional healing, and most days, I was a different man than my lover had first met.

New and improved—Jasper-approved.

I would choose him all over again to be the one who rescued me behind the hotel. There was no other voice I would have call out to send Joseph running. No other hands on my body to stop my bleeding. No other comforting touch I felt clear through to my soul. We had bonded in that back alley, and regardless of all the shit that had led us to that fateful night, I would gladly relive each and every moment since it had landed me at his side.

A rock the same as always, Jasper stood at my left, his warm palm pressed against my sweatier one. We'd combined our households a few days earlier and had dressed up for a dinner party.

Silas's assistant opened his and Troy's condo door. "Come on in, Mason. Jasper." She greeted us both with a smile. "Help yourselves to the bar and appetizers. Dinner will be served in about an hour."

We'd been invited as a welcome for his newest team, and it was the first time that I walked into a public setting free from the façade I'd worn for too long. After retrieving glasses of champagne from the kitchen bar, I greeted a couple of my co-workers, introducing Jasper as my partner. It felt good, and I was sure my face glowed.

"I'm so damn proud of you, baby," Jasper whispered as Silas and Troy approached us. "Even more, I'm blessed to be the one on your arm."

Of course, my eyes stung, but I managed to swallow back the tears in front of my boss.

"Mason." Tumbler in hand, a dapper-looking Silas greeted me with an authentic smile he didn't reveal too often.

"Silas." I released Jasper's hand to grasp Silas's, impressed and intimidated as always by the powerful aura he emanated. Still, I managed to be myself around him.

Troy stood beside him in a pink...blouse? that intensified his ethereal glow. Willowy and graceful, the gorgeous man could have starred as an elf in any movie set in Middle Earth. Jasper stared at the silky material with a yearning look as Troy greeted us.

Something tickled the back of my mind, jostling my memory from when I'd unpacked my clothing into Jasper's closet. I'd accidentally knocked over a stack of his shoe boxes. One lid had popped open, revealing a bit of similar material to Troy's shirt rather than the loafers I'd expected. I'd remembered Jasper's bottom drawer filled with panties at that moment and again wondered over why he hid that part of himself from me.

I considered the fact his father had been a bully. Called him a faggot. Had his treatment over the years caused Jasper to feel ashamed of his desires?

"Congratulations on your success," Troy said, pressing himself against Silas and bringing my focus on the present. Thoughts of feminine clothing and whatever wounds my boyfriend still secretly lugged around could wait until we had privacy.

"I wouldn't have it without you and Silas," I assured him. "Thank you."

"We're happy to have you on the payroll," Silas said, handing me a folded piece of paper.

Working for Silas was a dream come true. The other three people on my team seemed handpicked to act like a well-oiled machine—which we did. We had put together a long-term plan to drag a failing start-up business from the cliff of bankruptcy, and with Silas's slight tweaks and his Midas touch, he not only bailed them out but sold the company for a ridiculous profit.

I'd never seen a bonus check like the one I unfolded.

"Holy fuck." I gulped, focus jerking up to his appreciative gaze.

"Thank you for your hard work and dedication to making me money."

I barked a laugh at Silas's statement, loving the playful smirk that lessened his intensity. "Glad to be of service."

How often had I'd claimed those words earlier in the year while on the clock for Elite? Like my life at the time, the statement had been a lie. But with Silas? I'd never been more grateful to fulfill my role in his company. Sitting in an office and some days working remote from home satisfied me ten times more than feigning a persona and offering up my dick for some random guy who'd paid to be stuffed full.

Sure, my weekly hours for Silas tended to be triple if not quadruple of those with Elite, but I wouldn't have traded my new job for anything. A sense of accomplishment filled me on a daily basis, and with Jasper's dedication and love, as well as Zeke's continued therapy sessions, I enjoyed more emotional highs than lows.

The four of us stood and bullshitted for a little while before the elephant in the room became a topic of conversation. Leave it to the lawyer to mention Joseph's upcoming trial.

"Will you go?" Troy addressed me.

Jasper had asked me the same a few times. While I wanted to gloat in watching Joseph lose hope about escaping the charges against him, I had no wish to relive the night I'd been the one tied to a bed, drugged, and sexually assaulted.

Rarely did a day pass that I didn't have a memory flit through my brain about Joseph Delaney and all he'd done to me, but they no longer tilted me off my axis. I'd learned to redirect my thoughts when they became overwhelming thanks to Zeke and the "toolbox" he'd given me. I'd gained a level of stability I hadn't known existed, and I finally felt comfortable in my own skin. Learning to accept my feelings was a life-altering feat. Intentional shutdowns had become a thing of the past.

But facing Joseph could very well bring an emotional shitstorm I wasn't sure I could withstand.

I wanted to though. Fuck, how I lusted to hold his gaze, let him see that I'd found my footing, that Jasper continued to cradle the heart he'd attempted to carve his name into. Joseph had forced me to share his blood, but he would never own my soul in the way Jasper did.

My innermost parts as well as the physical body protecting them all belonged to my partner.

"I haven't decided yet," I said.

Jasper squeezed my hand, a silent assurance that he had my back no matter what I chose.

"Is Detective Jenner still after you to press charges?" Silas asked. "If they have a second man's almost identical story added atop the first victim, there's no way Delaney will be able to get his son another slap to the wrist rather than life behind bars."

"He just called again yesterday," I said, "but I haven't changed my answer."

Joseph's past record had come out in the media—drug possession, battery, and more than a few harassment orders against him. While Detective Jenner wasn't able to share details with me, I'd read through the lines during our phone conversations.

The death threat texts I'd received the night Joseph showed up at Jasper's were almost identical to the other victim's. The detective had hinted that a video also contained damning evidence—of myself showcased as a casualty of Joseph's unlawful kinks as well. I had been identified, but again I declared I wouldn't press charges. Nor would I take the stand.

Without my testimony or coming forward, Joseph would get twenty years at the least if found guilty of the District Attorney's charges. Was it enough?

Did he deserve to rot the rest of his days behind bars? Absolutely. But I was comfortable in the life I'd found. I just wanted to work, go home to the man I loved more than life, and crawl beneath the covers with him after cooking our dinner together.

Jasper didn't lean either way. He supported my decision, same as Micah.

"And the DA?" Troy asked. "Surely they would be pushing to get you on the stand if those videos you told us about showed your face."

"Reluctant witness," I stated, expecting he would understand since he knew about Elite. The defense would probably dig into my past and crush me to a bloody pulp. I'd done research since filing that order. It had been for the best I'd never gone after Joseph.

Shit *would* have hit the fan.

"So now what?" Silas asked, tugging Troy just a little tighter against his side.

"Now, I help my boss fill his bank coffers during the day and spend the rest of my time with my man."

Silas's eyes gleamed as though he understood the two desires I'd stated. "Here's to making both come true for countless years to come."

I clinked my champagne glass to his tumbler, hoping his toast manifested itself.

Chapter 26

Jasper

"So damn proud of you," I told Mason, fumbling with the buttons of his shirt. Usually, I took my time while undressing him, but I'd been on edge.

"You've said that about ten times tonight," Mason claimed with a soft chuckle, his words slightly slurred. He'd had quite a bit of champagne, but even before he'd caught a buzz, his eyes had remained unshuttered, open and vulnerable. He'd been himself while socializing at Silas and Troy's. And I loved him for it. Needed to show him how much.

Shoving his shirt off his shoulders, I leaned in and swept my tongue over his scar that had finally healed over. Only a slight puckered line of skin revealed the *J*, but I'd claimed it as my own. I closed my teeth over Mason's nipple, tugging.

"Ah!" He gulped, hands grasping my head as his button-down slipped to the floor. "Fuck, that hurts."

I repeated the action since Mason enjoyed a little pain on occasion. "You're so damn hot, baby." Hands attacking his belt, I slid to my knees. "Want to worship you. Suck you until you come on my tongue."

"Shit," Mason whispered, staring down at me, pupils blown. "Yeah—do that."

Slacks around his ankles, he groaned as I licked up the back of his hard cock to the beaded pearl of pre-cum at his slit. He hissed, and I swallowed him to the root.

Curses spilled from his lips, and he widened his knees the best he could as I toyed over his taint with my fingertips. "Want one—give it to me."

Such a needy hole my man had. I fucking loved it.

Index slathered in spit, I swallowed him once more and relented, going straight for his sweet spot.

"Oh yes. Right there, Jasper. So good." He gulped audibly, and I glanced up to find his focus on me, tongue flicking over his lower lip. "Love you so much."

Knowing he could see my echoed reply in my eyes, I held his gaze and gave him the blow job of his life. His legs shook, and his entire body shuddered, bucking against our front door when he filled my mouth with his cum.

I swallowed it down. Licked him clean, then offered him my tongue so he could taste himself on me.

FF
MM

We showered together the next morning, quiet and thorough in cleaning each other, but didn't linger since we both had to work, and our time ran short.

After toweling off, I went to Mason's bureau to pick his clothes for the day, but he grasped my wrist. "Change of pace this morning."

"What's that, baby?" I asked.

Mason studied my face with anxiety welling in his eyes.

I frowned. "Mase?"

"Will...will you allow me to dress you today?" His face flushed from our hot shower, his hair a damp and riotous mess I smoothed back. He leaned into my touch as always, but the troubled look in his eyes remained.

"If you'd like," I murmured, since he obviously needed to take care of me in that moment.

"I would." He led me to the foot of our bed, and I sat, offering him a reassuring smile.

"Do you trust me?" he asked quietly, his gaze somewhat intense.

I leaned forward and kissed his stomach when I would rather have questioned him. "You know I do."

Mason released a slow exhale. "Stay here." He headed toward our walk-in closet, but it wouldn't be a difficult choice for him. I tended toward blue shirts in all shades, and simple ties to go with my suits.

I glanced at the clock as he took forever beyond my line of sight. We didn't have much time before—

The thought of being late for work shot from my mind as Mason emerged with a piece of clothing I hadn't looked at or touched for months. Pale pink silk spilled over his shaking hands, and my heart stumbled, the blood draining from my face.

No, no, no—

"Arms up," he whispered, his focus on my chest as he held the nightie by its spaghetti straps.

I swallowed hard at the memory of the last time its hem had brushed over the middle of my thighs. "Mase..."

"Please." He still stared at where my heart threatened to burst from my body.

Unsure of what to think or even try to read his mind or intent, I released an unsteady exhale and gave him what he wanted.

He slid the silken material over my head, the sheath fluttering to pool around my waist.

"Don't move," he murmured and hurried to the bedstand.

Fuck.

How long had he known?

Fists at my sides, I chewed on the inside of my lip until I tasted blood. I swallowed repeatedly as Mason knelt before me with my favorite lace panties. He didn't speak but caressed my ankle until I lifted first one foot then the other for him to slide them on. Hands still shaking, he slid the scrap of material up to my knees.

"Stand up for me?" he whispered with a hint of a question in his voice.

Regardless of my trembling legs, I obeyed, the towel falling from my waist to the floor, the shift drifting down to cover my cock and balls.

My lover pulled the panties up my hairy thighs, settling the waistband into place. Without a word, he took my hand and led me to the full-length mirror tucked into the corner of our bedroom.

Refusing to look at myself, I studied Mason's reflection where he stood behind me.

He slid his fingertips over my shoulders, toying with the straps of the nightie. Holding my gaze in the mirror, he smoothed my palms along my sides to my waist where he began to bunch up the soft material, slowly baring my groin.

A low groan escaped him. "So damn pretty—look at you, Jasper."

I gulped at his words, the awe in his tone.

He didn't think I was a sick pervert...

Wetness welled in my eyes as he held the nightie at my waist, his other hand slipping down to cup my lace-covered bulge. He kissed my shoulder before licking up my neck. One step brought him closer, pressing the evidence of what my appearance did to his body against me.

"You—you aren't disgusted?" I rasped.

"No."

"T-Triggered?" I asked, thinking about the clothing Joseph had worn the night he'd taken advantage of my love.

Mason was quiet for a few moments, but I saw the second he figured out exactly what I'd asked. "Not even a tiny bit." He ground his dick against my ass. "See how perfect you are?" he whispered against my ear before stroking his tongue over the shell and sending shivers down my spine. "Every inch of you, inside and out. You're the present wrapped up in a pretty pink bow I always dreamed about as a young boy and never received."

A tear slid down my cheek, and he turned me toward him, gathering me into his arms.

"I love you, Jasper. Every part—and if you want to dress like this at home, hell, even when we go out on dates, I'm here for it. Want it, even. I'm having sudden fantasies about you tucking that lace off to the side before you wreck my ass."

"You don't think that's...weird? It's normally the bottom wearing panties or thongs."

He snorted. "No fucking way." He ground his groin against mine, enticing my dick to thicken up. "Does that feel like the thought of my pretty top wearing fem clothing turns me off?"

A soft, shaky laugh escaped me, and I finally wrapped my arms around his neck, leaning into the precious moment I couldn't believe was reality.

"You know what would be really sexy?" He grabbed my ass and squeezed.

"Hmm?" I toyed with the hair at the nape of his neck, completely and utterly gone on my man.

"Mascara on your eyelashes. Blush on your cheekbones, and gloss on your lips."

My inhale snagged.

"Is that something you would like?" he murmured, once more studying my face.

"Fuck, Mase." More tears welled in my eyes. "Yes," I choked on the word.

He wrapped his arms tighter around me. "Will you tell me why you've felt the need to hide this side of yourself from me?"

I tipped my forehead against his chin, eyes clenched, and breathed steadily until I calmed enough to speak. "One of my earliest memories was from kindergarten when my father mocked my tears over having to wear a collared shirt for my first school picture. Green and blue...with three buttons. I'd put on a fuchsia blouse from my mother's closet and had gone down for breakfast, excited over how pretty I looked.

"He'd ripped it off me. Reminded me that I was a *boy*. It was the first time I heard the word faggot and that I was nothing more than a waste of his seed."

Mason made a low, pained sound in his throat.

"My mother cowered in the kitchen's corner rather than protecting me or speaking up in my defense," I continued, unable to hide the continuing hurt from my voice. "In all the years that followed, she never corrected whenever he said I had no value, no worth, as a son. That school picture hung on prominent display in my parent's living room, my father's reminder of what he expected of his only child. I burned the image the night he passed."

"I'm so fucking sorry you went through that."

I heaved a heavy exhale. "There was no forgiveness or reconciliation between us due to years of verbal, emotional, and physical abuse."

"Look at you now," he murmured and kissed my forehead. "You've not just risen above the ashes like a glorious phoenix, but you've turned death into something achingly gorgeous. I wouldn't change a damned thing about you. And as for being useless?" He snorted. "You brought me back from the edge of barely living. You've filled my life with happiness and love. I couldn't survive a day without you, Jasper. You're necessary to me. I'm going to cherish and hoard you away where only I can touch you for years to come."

My throat tightened up again.

I'd been stuck beneath my father's influence, unable to get out from beneath the memory of his conditional love. He'd kept me from living long after he rotted in the ground.

But Mason...

He'd become my savior—so I dropped to my knees to worship him, work be damned.

Chapter 27

Jasper

Mason's and my relationship thrived as the summer days gave way to cooler apple-picking weather. We met together with Zeke on a weekly basis, working side by side on our continued emotional healing.

He made friends outside Elite, mostly his co-workers in Silas's company, but with Zeke's husband Levi as well. We'd had them over for dinner a few times and vice versa. Mason even began volunteering at Humanity House on Tuesday nights.

As for me?

I embraced the desires I'd kept secret for far too long all due to a man who could no longer hurt me. While I saved the mascara and more feminine clothing for enjoyment in the privacy of our home, I wore pretty panties every day beneath my suits, every morning whispering a big *FUCK YOU* in my mind. I used gloss to keep my lips moist. I even gave up the more masculine deodorant and body spray for something lighter and more feminine.

The best news had come in mid-September. Mason's

brother-in-law had gotten a new job with insurance that would cover the cost of Mason's nephew's need for constant care and medical treatments. A burden had lifted off my lover's shoulders, and I cried tears along with him while he FaceTimed with his sister.

No one had noticed—or had chosen not to mention—the mascara tracks on my cheeks or the fact a purple negligee hung off one of my shoulders when I couldn't keep from moving onscreen to offer my congratulations in person.

Mason had wondered once upon a time if Marin's family loved him, but there was no denying the emotions on their faces. Smiling, eyes shining, they crowded Marin's cell screen to better see him, both boys begging for him to visit until their mom grew annoyed and told them to quiet down.

My heart ached for Mason, and I couldn't help but feel a little jealous he had family who seemed to adore him.

I promised him that someday soon we would fly to Montana to finally meet his brother-in-law and nephews in person and spend time with them.

Mason and Kellen remained close regardless of his quitting Elite. I'd heard that sparks flew between Detective Jenner—JJ—and Kellen. They definitely had something going on, but Mason's friend gave vague answers whenever he got nosey.

My lover and Kellen had spent the day together, something I'd insisted Mason do every couple of weeks.

Outside work, Mason and I were attached at the hip. He needed to be himself sometimes, not "Mason with Jasper" every second of the day. When I'd first insisted on time away from each other, he'd been devastated—until he figured out that I merely wanted him to know who he was when I wasn't around.

My feelings for him wouldn't change, and I'd felt confident that our love would only grow since neither of us carried around secrets any longer.

I'd been proven right.

Whenever Mason went out with his co-workers or friends, he returned a hungry man, begging for my attention. He even initiated contact on occasion, and I enjoyed every second of him being in charge. But when it came time for gratification, he always gave over and let me lead.

Fuck, did I love him.

Saturday night, he came in after hanging with Kellen since early afternoon. Pink flushed his cheeks, lust lit his eyes, and I expected him to fall on me where I sat on the couch in a silk robe covered in butterflies.

I eyed him as he moved toward me, noting how his hand clenched and relaxed at his sides like he milked a damn cow. "Everything okay, baby?"

His head jerked up and down.

Something was definitely off, but I kept silent until he stood before me. He stared at me, unease in his gaze, his feet shifty—but inner peace still rolled from him.

I took his hand, threading my fingers with his since he seemed to need help grounding himself.

"Make love to me?" he asked, his voice a thready whisper.

Standing, I slid my other hand to his nape, drawing him closer. He sagged against me as our mouths brushed. The sweetness of his breath, the softness of his whiskers, raised a sigh from my lungs.

Comfort and deep yearning wound together in an unbreakable bond between us, making me hunger to bring him pleasure.

We broke apart, and I led him to our bedroom, flicking off the living room and kitchen lights on our way.

He stood at the foot of our bed, hands once more clenched at his sides as I shut our door.

Rather than ask what had him unsettled, I moved in close to strip him down, knowing my attention and touch would calm his inner anxiety. I grasped the hem of his T-shirt.

He shivered.

I lifted and paused at his chest uncovered. "Mase—" My voice broke, and I quickly tore his shirt off the rest of the way and dropped it to the floor.

Jasper was spelled out in scripted ink over his heart.

He swallowed audibly as I traced my shaking fingertip over the letters of my name. "I didn't want the reminder of him on my skin anymore," Mason whispered. "What he'd meant for evil, I turned into something beautiful. Your name is etched on my heart, my soul—and now on my skin for the world to see."

My throat tightened. I couldn't speak.

"D-Do you hate it?"

I shook my head quickly. "No—no, I don't hate it—fuck, Mase. Baby." A tear slid down my cheek, and I leaned in, kissing the covered scar I'd shown love to every time we came together. He'd tattooed my name on his skin. Permanently.

Fuck, I wanted to do the same.

I undressed my lover the rest of the way until he stood before me, shivering and so damn needy his dick leaked. I shed my robe, and kissing his mouth, I walked forward until the bed hit the back of his knees. We tumbled onto the mattress, both of us moaning as our bodies caressed chest to feet.

"Love you," I murmured, trailing my mouth along his neck.

A shiver slid over him as I sucked on his clavicle hard enough to leave a slight mark. He groaned, shifting his hips to press his cock against my satin-covered one.

I licked to his other side, marking his skin there as well.

His nipples received a fair bit of attention, and I left them reddened and slightly puffy.

Mason panted for breath beneath me, his dick hard as rock, balls already tightened against his groin. I loved on the latter, using my mouth to tug them away from his body. I nibbled on his taint. Licked over his hole.

"Jasper," he pleaded with me, but I took my time stretching him out with first my tongue, then with lubed fingers.

His erection didn't flag even as I pushed three inside him, pressing deep to make room for my dick.

Our gazes locked, desire a living entity between us.

He lifted his hips, using my fingers to fuck himself. "Ready for you—please. Need you inside me, Jasper."

I withdrew from his body and wiped myself clean on sheets we would definitely need to change before going to bed. I planned on making a mess.

Scooting up to lounge against the headboard, I shoved my panties off to the side and held my dick by its base so it stood upright toward the ceiling. "Suck me."

A gleam lit in Mason's eyes as he rolled and attached his mouth to my glans. He lathed and suckled, his gaze on me the entire time.

"So good, baby." I ran my fingers through his hair, holding in place so he could be in charge.

The give and take between us was like an ocean wave, sometimes crashing, sometimes gentle laps on the shore—

but always a steady flow back and forth, the same as nature's beauty. There could be no certainty of continuance without both motions.

Teeth clenched, I sat still rather than fucking into his throat like my body lusted for. He gave me pleasure, and I took all he had to offer, storing every loving stroke of his tongue in my memory for the moments I missed him throughout the day.

I approached the edge too quickly, and I tugged him up by his hair. Mason crawled over my body on hands and knees. Our mouths came together with hunger—wet kisses and low moans.

"Want you on my dick, baby," I whispered against his mouth, loving how dirty talk made him shudder. "Want to fuck up into your tight hole with long, slow strokes until you paint my abs with your cum."

"Jasper." His eyelids fell shut.

I slapped his ass to yank him from the brink of blowing without my cock up his ass and hand on his dick.

He hissed and grabbed hold of my spit-slickened length. Shifting, he settled the flared head of my shaft against his hole. I'd shoved enough lube up inside he had no issue filling himself with one steady push back.

The second his cheeks met my groin, he clenched around my girth.

"Ah, fuck." I grasped his hips to keep him still.

"Payback is a bitch," he murmured with a smirk while draping his forearms around my neck.

"Come here, baby."

He listened as always, giving me his mouth, and feet planted on the mattress, I began fucking in and out of him with the promised languid pace that drove him crazy.

"Feels so silky inside your ass," I told him between

kisses. "You fit me perfectly—your hole is so damn greedy for my dick."

"Yes," he moaned, tearing his mouth from mine.

Foreheads tipped together, we shared breaths as the wet schlicking sounds of our love echoed through the bedroom. With every unrushed thrust of my hips, I ran my hands over his back. Trailed fingertips down his spine. Grasped his ass cheeks in my palms.

I neared the edge of climax but wasn't yet ready for the moment to end.

"Sit up—ride me."

Mason straightened, his hands on my chest, hips swiveling and lifting as I fought to breathe steady and hold still. His hard dick swayed and bobbed, dribbling pre-cum down his long length.

Such a gorgeous dick.

"Touch me," he begged, his tone nothing but gravel.

"Need to come, baby?"

"Yes. So badly."

Left hand atop his heart, the gift of his tattoo, I took him in my right, jacking in time with his swiveling hips. "Want to come like this, Mase—slow torture."

"Jasper," he whined, grabbing my left wrist with both his hands to keep mine against his chest.

"Work your sweet spot with my dick," I murmured, thumbing over his glans.

He shifted his knees higher, leaning back slightly.

"Yes," I hissed, "take your pleasure from me, Mase. Give me your orgasm."

"Jasper—fuck." He gulped, and I thrust up to meet him. "M-More—please."

He attempted to ride me harder. Faster.

Lifting our hands to his neck, I grasped lightly. "*Slow,*" I reminded him, and he whimpered again, a pitiful, needy sound that caused my sac to tighten.

I stroked his length in time with his lifting hips, snapping mine when he bottomed out. Pre-cum slickened my palm, and I rubbed over his swollen head with every upward tug.

"Talk dirty to me," he gasped as his thighs began to quiver.

"Clench that hole around my dick." I swore when he obeyed. "Fuck, yes—you were made for me, baby. Your ass is so damn hot and wet inside. Wanna fuck the cum right out of you."

"Yes—" He gulped, slamming down onto my length.

"Gonna breed you. Fill you up," I whispered the words through clenched teeth. "Unload so far into your hole you're going to be dripping for days."

"Oh fuck." Mason's eyelids popped open, and his blown pupils stole my goddamn breath. "You're gonna make me come—"

His dick bucked in my hand, and cum spurted over my chest.

"Yes, baby—yes." I slammed up into his tight heat as my balls convulsed, shooting my spunk deep in his ass.

Mason fell forward, our mouths crashing together. We swallowed each other's groans as our cocks continued to pulse their release.

My ears rang. Heart fucking raced.

I couldn't drive deep enough, couldn't reach clear through to his soul so I could lay claim to what I wanted for life.

His cum smeared between our bodies as I wrapped my arms around him, holding on tight. Eventually, our frantic movements slowed to gentle rocking and soft kisses. We came to a rest, a sweat and cum slickened mess.

My seed dripped from his ass around my softening dick, dripping off my balls to the bed below.

Still, we didn't move.

"You're the greatest gift I could ever imagine," I told him, one arm clasped around his waist, the other hand's fingers trailing through his hair. "Thank you for loving me."

He kissed my neck where he'd tucked his head, his whiskers sending shivers down my arms. "My pleasure."

Epilogue

Mason

The cold, November wind bit at our faces as we slipped out of the courthouse's back exit. Hands clasped tightly, we hurried toward Jasper's car, bypassing people making for the front where a crowd probably waited for word from the District Attorney and his team.

Neither of us spoke.

I hadn't been a basket case like both Jasper and I had expected while watching Joseph wait for his fate. I hadn't shut down, nor had I donned my fake persona in the courtroom. I'd chosen to face my past and had done so with a steady stare, unwavering and unmoved. On the outside, at least.

While I'd come a hell of a long way in a few short months thanks to Jasper's love and Zeke's help, I still struggled with my emotions on occasion.

Jasper had sat beside me, holding my hand every day as we had listened to the District Attorney's office go into great detail about Joseph Delaney's crimes against the original victim to press charges. A second had come forward before the trial had begun—Joseph's first obsession. Same as myself and the last man tied to Joseph's bed, he had a J-shaped scar on his chest. And the same as the others, he'd been forcibly intoxicated and sexually assaulted by a young man dressed in a tutu and sparkly fairy wings.

Jasper had cringed at hearing the described attire, shifting his ass on the hard bench we sat upon. I'd glanced at him, but he'd feigned a smile to put me at ease. I'd leaned in and pressed my lips to his forehead assuring him that I *was* fine, that no piece of clothing he chose to put on his body would trigger my PTSD.

The first victim of Joseph's morbid actions had gone to the hospital and had blood drawn to prove he'd been drugged. Rather than seeking out the authorities, he'd taken his evidence to Joseph's father and had accepted a large settlement to keep quiet. He'd remained silent until the latest victim went after the young man who'd hurt them both.

The District Attorney had played the videos Joseph had saved on his laptop of the two incidents, vivid, high-def recordings of what he'd done to the men. Detective Jenner had informed me that my assault had been recorded as well, but the DA didn't expose me or my video to the court.

Jurors had been green around the gills, and I'd had to close my eyes when Joseph had cut himself and leaned over the other two men he'd taken advantage of to smear his blood with theirs atop their chests. At least they'd pixelated private parts and kept the sound muted. Joseph's words, however, had been written out verbatim, read aloud.

We had watched Detective Jenner take the stand, laying out all the evidence he and his team had gathered. We listened as a forensic expert spoke of DNA on the boar's head knife that matched the first victim.

My DNA had been the second found, but again, had not been mentioned or named.

While the defense's closing argument begged for leniency for young Joseph, the attorney's words had fallen on deaf ears thanks to the DA's solid case. Joseph had created his own noose and not just with the video. There had been hundreds of damning messages and voice messages too.

It had been a slam dunk from day one, but he'd been arrogant enough to think he could win, refusing to plead guilty for a lesser sentence or claim insanity.

A couple nightmares haunted me during the lengthy trial, but Jasper kept me from floundering. He'd been my rock through every hour, staying by my side with every day that passed.

And now it's over.

Jasper and I climbed into the car, and he turned the heat on blast mode, holding his hands to his mouth to exhale hot air over them.

I buckled in and sat still, hands in my lap, staring out the windshield, my mind finally resting thanks to the privacy we shared.

"You okay, baby?" He reached over and threaded his fingers through mine.

A slow smile curved my lips. "Yes."

My attacker, the young man who'd stalked me and nearly ended my life, had been found guilty on all charges. The judge's expression had held a note of satisfaction in hearing the verdict read before the court.

Joseph was given life in prison with no chance of parole for how he'd scarred the two men's minds, their memories, and their bodies. He might have been used by fate to gift me the love of a lifetime that humid night back in July, but I took great pleasure in knowing he'd been brought lower than sewer rats.

He would have no money for pretty clothes.

No salon for those golden curls.

No designer jumpsuit to set him apart from the other criminals he would be surrounded by.

I wished some massive, STD-ridden inmate would make Joseph his sex slave. I wanted him to be rough and get off on Joseph's tears. Maybe tie him up. Take a knife to him just for fun. I hoped the little shit lived a miserable-ever-after beneath a beast of terror hellbent on ripping him in two without lube every damn night for the rest of his worth-less life.

My thoughts bordered sadistic and cruel, but I believed people ought to reap what they sowed. Eye for an eye and all that shit. Joseph Delaney the third deserved pain and terror. I prayed karma made him her bitch.

I slowly emptied my lungs and sent along thoughts concerning Joseph's future from my mind along with my exhale. He was our past.

Jasper and I had one hell of a future ahead of us.

"I'm glad it's over," I finally murmured after fifteen minutes of silent driving. I glanced over to find Jasper smil-ing. He lifted our clasped hands and kissed my knuckles.

"I've been making strides toward creating a new life," I continued, "and with your help, I've achieved a ton. But now?" I squeezed his fingers tight, rubbing my thumb over the back of his hand in a gentle caress. "He is nothing more than a thing from my past. There's no chance of running into him on the street, no way my cell will ever light up with a threatening text. His obsession might remain, but I'm truly free of it."

As though to mock me, my cell dinged a notification.

I swiped the screen and grinned. "Micah sent me a *Fuck yes!*" I chuckled. "Guess the news just broke."

My cell pinged again.

Another huff of delight left me at seeing my best friend's message. "Kellen said the exact same thing."

Jasper gave me my hand back so I could reply to my friends.

Micah had kept in touch with me regardless of my leaving Elite. We'd even been invited for a huge Thanksgiving after-party at his massive home. Kellen planned to attend as well, and I couldn't wait to show off my lover in the new blouse and billowy pants I'd bought for him. His usual loafers would remain in our closet in exchange for a pair of heeled boots I'd begged him to fuck me in the week before the trial had started.

Jasper pulled into our parking spot, and I was ready to get comfortable and sit down with my boyfriend to relax after one hell of an emotional day.

Too tired for sex, we settled onto our couch with glasses of wine in hand. I sat in the corner, a knee bent toward Jasper and lightly resting atop his thigh. While Yo-Yo Ma played Bach quietly in the background, we discussed our upcoming vacation to the Cayman Islands. Ten days of quietness. No stress. No jobs. Nothing to think about but our future.

Jasper had informed me he'd made plans to escape Boston and winter once the trial ended, and I hadn't argued. While the trip had dented our savings, my raise and Silas's generosity in bonuses meant our dream home fund would quickly amass to a decent down payment once we decided to start looking for our forever home.

"So we have a stop to make before we head to the

airport on Black Friday," Jasper said, swirling his wine and staring at it.

"Oh?" I sipped my drink, unable to tear my eyes off my boyfriend in his favorite butterfly robe. The dark pink of the soft material matched the color rising in his cheeks.

"The courthouse."

My smile faded, brow furrowing slightly.

Jasper set his wine on the coffee table and slid to the floor beside me, fishing in his robe's pocket. "You gave me your heart, Mason, but I want you to take my last name as well."

My gaze ensnared on the ring he held up between two fingers, the reality of what he did crashing into me like a ten foot swell, stealing my breath. My throat attempted to close off. "Jasper," I choked out his name.

"Say yes, baby," he whispered, his sweet amber eyes full of devotion and love. "Make me the happiest man on the damn planet."

Tears welled in my eyes as I offered him my left hand. "Yes."

He slid the ring where it belonged and pressed up to kiss my lips. "All it had taken was one night for me to know I wanted you forever."

My heart melted. "And now you'll have me."

THE END

About the Author

USA Today bestselling author Lynn Burke is a CrossFit and coffee addict. Her three spawn dictate how often she can be found hunched over her Mac, typing as fast as her fickle muse cooks up hot stories.

You can find more about Lynn at her website: www. authorlynnburke.com

Also By Lynn Burke

Abel's Obsession

Divulging Secrets

Healing Storms

In Between

Reluctant Lumberjack

Resisting his Mate

Billion Dollar Love Anthology

Blood Born Series

Bonds of Worship Series

Dark Leopards MC

Darkest Desires Series

Devil's Outlaws MC

Elite Escort Series

Elite Escorts MM Series

Fallen Gliders MC

Forbidden Obsession Duet

Found by Fate Series

Midnight Sun Series

Missing Link Series

Risso Family Series

Sandy Ridge Series

Sinful Nature Series

Vicious Vipers MC